日本人

幽默人物百選

**OBSERVATIONS BY
TIM ERNST
AND
MIKE MARKLEW**

監修：張思本
譯者：鄺宗明

編 者 的 話

　　了解一個國家或是學習語言時，除了教科書之外，也可藉多方面來加快學習的腳步。東漢日語文化中心本身因爲從事語言的教育，我們也希望藉由各個的角度去觀察日本，因此推出了日本系列叢書。第一本「日本－姿與心」承蒙全國各大公司及學校列爲學習參考用書，廣受好評，系列中的第二本「日語中的關鍵語」，也確實的帶給許多讀者在學習時先了解日語的關鍵用語及基礎知識上有所助益；且全書附上平假名，減少讀者查閱字典的時間，並能有效的充實語彙的能力。

　　本書「日本鳥人」爲本日本系列中的第三冊，這本書的作者爲英美人士，用他們幽默的角度去觀察日本社會，發現了許多有趣的現象，但是在細讀之下，也發現台灣也有許多類似的「鳥族」如「新人類」、「暴走族（飆車族）」等，除了會心而笑之外，反令人深思不已。

　　當然本書也和其他本系列的叢書一般，希望讀者除了吸取新知之外，且能夠充實語文方面的知識，因此採取了「中、英、日」三國語言的對譯方式，藉由不同語言的角度，來了解各個語言的表現。當然如果可以運用這些幽默話題及字彙，相信可增加說話的幽默感，增進人際關係。

　　因此本書的最主要的著眼點，是希望大眾在了解不同的文化及社會的前提下，又能達到學習的目的。當然本書詼諧的語調，也許會令其他人士感到不悅，但是在這請大家多多包涵作者的出發點及其角度。

　　最後，我們要特別感謝作者 Tim Ernst 及 Mike Marklew 及 Japan Times 出版事業局齊藤純一局長，他們爽朗的答應並鼎力支持本書的出版，特此申謝。

編 者 謹 誌 於
東 漢 文 化 中 心

Disclaimer

This book is intended to be a humorous depiction of Japanese society at large, without any malice toward anybody. Except for the caricatures of the authors (Observers) and those of their children (WAA Children), any resemblance to persons living or dead of the characters depicted herein, is purely coincidental. All caricatures and characters in this book are fictitious, the product of the author(s)' imagination. No attempt was made to stereotype, degrade or belittle any profession, member of either sex, or peculiarities inherent in any society. References of an ornithological nature were made merely to add humor to the descriptions and to give the book the "sense" of a zoological field guide. We apologize in advance to anyone offended by our book. We apologize to any birds as well. It is our fervent hope that all will laugh and enjoy reading this book as much as we have laughed and enjoyed making it.

The authors

おことわり

　本書は日本社会全般をユーモラスに描いたもので、特定の個人に対する悪意はありません。著者自身とその子供達がモデルの「日本人ウォッチャー」と「『ハーフ』の子供たち」以外は、実在の人物に似せたものではありません。本書における人物描写はすべてフィクション、すなわち著者の想像の産物であり、特定の職業・性別・ある社会の特異性を中傷・差別・誹謗する意図はまったくありません。ユーモアと動物図鑑の雰囲気を本書に与えるため、鳥類になぞらえた描写もしました。この本によって気分を害された方々には、前もってここでお詫びします。トリたちにもお詫びします。我々が本書を書くにあたって大いに笑い、楽しんだのと同様、読者の皆様が大いに笑い、楽しんでくださることを望んでやみません。

著者一同

前言

　　本書是以幽默的手法來描述日本整體社會，對於特定的人物沒有絲毫的惡意。除了「日本觀察家」及「混血兒」是以作者及其小孩爲模特兒外，其餘都不是素描現實中的人物。本書中的人物全屬虛構，同時也是作者想像的產物，因此本書沒有對於特定的職業、性別、或是某個社會的特異性有任何惡意中傷、歧視、誹謗的意圖。爲了賦予幽默感及有動物圖鑑的味道，因此以鳥類爲對象，加以臨摹、描繪。若因本書的任何不妥之處，使得讀者有任何不愉快時，在此先行致歉。同時也向鳥兒們說聲對不起。我們在製作此書時，曾放聲大笑，非常愉快，也希望讀者與我們一般，同樣享受這份愉快，一同放聲笑呵呵。

作者一同

"A society without humor
is no laughing matter."

〔タクシーの運転手〕

すこぶる礼儀正しく、チップを要求する性質はない。もし日本語でちょっとでも話しかけられようものなら、えんえんとおしゃべりを続けるのも特徴。いたるところ無数に生息するが、雨の日と深夜～午前3時に捕獲するのは困難である。彼らの巣はきわめて清潔に保たれている。しばしば自動ドアでガイジンを痛い目にあわせる事は、つとに有名。意図的ではないようだが....。

《計程車司機族》

行為舉止非常得體，且彬彬有禮，從未要求小費。其特徵是只要你用日本話向他搭訕，話匣子一開就說個不停。足跡遍佈各地，但是特別在雨天或深夜到凌晨三點，非常難以「捕獲」。他們的「巢」總是保持得非常乾淨整潔，但常因自動門致外國人受害而有名。當然這並非其所願。

The Taxi Driver

Unusually polite and don't ask for tips. Often talk too much if you say anything in Japanese. Can read signs, but tend to get lost. Found everywhere in abundant supply but difficult to catch when raining or between midnight and 3 a.m. Nests are scrupulously clean. Have been known to unintentionally maim foreigners with their automatic doors!

〔アルバイター〕

　ファーストフード・チェーンの日本上陸（前ディズニーランド時代）と共に繁殖した人種。暗号的英語をあやつり、男性でもカン高い声を張り上げる。決して10代以上の年齢には見えないこの種族、スキーシーズンと夏休みには日本アルプスやらハワイやらへ移動する習性あり。しかるに1か月後、小麦色の肌に変貌している。年間を通し、異常に活動的である。

《打工族》

　　與速食連鎖店登陸日本（狄斯耐樂園時代之前）一起大量繁殖的人種。使用暗號般的英語，連男生也常高聲嘶喊。這個種族你絕看不出是由乳臭未乾的十幾歲娃兒們所組成。常有在滑雪季節或是夏季前往日本阿爾卑斯山或是去夏威夷度假的習性。一個月後，膚色會逐漸變爲小麥般的顏色。整年中總是精力旺盛的活動著。

The Arubaito (Part Timer)

Spawned by the arrival of fast food chains (pre-Disneyland), they speak in a form of coded English and even the males have ultra-high pitched voices. Never appear to be older than their teens, this breed changes color from pale to darkly tanned for one month after the ski season and summer holiday season when they migrate to the Japanese Alps or Hawaii respectively. Always effervescent.

〔OL〕

昼間はたいていスーツ姿なので見分けられるが、夜間になると識別しがたい。ランチタイムに一群となって出歩く習性がある。主な活動はお茶くみ・灰皿やゴミ箱のそうじ・封筒のあて名書き・文書の漢字タイプ・電話と来客の応対など。管理職につく者はまれで、多くは結婚退職していく。

《OL族》

白天大半都穿著制服很容易辨認，但是晚間則很難識別。有在午餐時間成群結隊出外遊走的習性。主要的工作是倒茶、清潔煙灰缸、廢紙簍、寫寫信封的地址、繕打公文、接電話與招呼客人。大部份都不會成為管理幹部，結婚後就辭職求去。

The O.L.

Usually be-suited in daylight, but difficult to distinguish at night. Swarm at lunchtime. All have startlingly straight hair and never smoke in the office. Specialize in making tea or coffee, emptying ashtrays and garbage bins, handwriting envelopes, typing letters in *kanji*, answering the telephone and greeting arriving visitors. Rarely reach executive status—most often get married and quit.

〔平均的サラリーマン〕

朝方、寝ボケまなこで群れをなしているから、発見はたやすい。社章バッジを付けたねずみ色の背広にワイシャツのいでたち。ニンニク臭のキツイ者も多いので注意すべし。すでにつがいになっている者は最低2時間通勤に費やすため、平日は夜も外食が多い。週末には昼ごろまで寝ていたり家族とドライブという「家族サービス」なる行動を取る。大学を出るや否やねずみ色に変色し、皆タバコを吸う人種である。

《一般上班族》

　　早上總是成群睡眼惺忪，因此很容易發現他們的蹤跡。服裝總是襯衫及訂著公司證章的灰色西裝，可要注意的是，有的人口中充滿著大蒜味。已婚者因爲通勤就要花費兩小時以上，平時及晚上都是在外覓食者較多。行動樣式是週末一覺睡到中午，或是常以開車兜風的方式來慰勞家族成員。不論是否大學出身，畢業後都搖身一變成爲灰衣族群，且多數是吸菸族。

The "Average" Salaryman

Easily seen in vast sleepy hordes in the morning. All wear dark suits with company lapel badge and white shirts. Beware of those who smell of garlic. Married ones often spend at least two hours every day travelling, rarely eat at home on weeknights and at weekends perform "famirii sābisu" by sleeping in late or taking the family out in their cars. Become prematurely grey on leaving university and all smoke cigarettes.

〔ビジネスマンと「娘」と称する女〕

　お高そうな喫茶店やブティック、さらには超高級レストランやホテルのロビー・温泉・列車の「特別席（グリーン車）」などで見かけられる人々。人前ではよそよそしいくらいに振る舞い、たいていひそひそ声で話している。男は会社の重役などが多く、「娘」と称する方はそうではないようだ。

《生意人與「妹妹」》

　　在一些高級咖啡廳及服飾店或是超高級的餐廳及飯店的大廳、溫泉休閒地區及電車的頭等艙中，常可看到這種家族。在大庭廣眾前，表現得不怎麼親熱，且都是輕聲細語。而男性大部份是公司的高級幹部，「妹妹」的那一位，看起來並不像是女兒喔。

The Businessman and "Daughter"

Found in exclusive coffee houses, expensive boutiques, even more expensive restaurants, hotel lobbies or spas and in the "Superior Seating" (Green Seat) cars of the bullet trains, they never touch each other in public and communication is usually in lowered voices. The males are most often corporate executives and their "daughters" are not.

〔早朝練習に励むプロ志望の野球選手〕

明け方から野球の素振りに没頭する集団をよく見るが、これはジョギングの日本版ともいえるもの。この野球熱は父親がテレビの野球中継を見すぎていたことによる先天性のもの、と唱える人類学者もいる。だが別の学説によれば、世の中、特に上司や義母への反抗心の表れという。

《黎明即起勤奮練習以參加職棒爲第一志願的選手》

破曉時分，常可見到許多認真練習棒球的集團，就像其他國家慢跑人們的日本版。也有人類學者指稱這份對棒球的熱愛，是源自於看多了電視實況轉播的父親的先天性遺傳。但是也有其他學者指出，這是反抗上司或丈母娘心態的表現。

The Early Morning Aspiring Baseball Star

Can be found by dawn's light on any vacant tract of land or rooftop, performing a Japanese club swinging ritual, which has become the native version of jogging. Some anthropologists claim this baseball ritual is instilled at birth by their fathers watching too many TV ballgames, however others believe it comes from a strong desire to "strike out" at society in general or their boss and mother-in-law in particular.

〔ボンサイスト〕

　あらゆる木を小人サイズに作り変える専門家。人々の住む家があまりに小さく庭もろくにないこの地では、不可欠な存在とされる。なぜならタタミにふとんで寝ていれば、盆栽の松の木であっても見上げることができるからだ。みかんの木を盆栽にすると実はまずくて食べられる代物ではないが、花はたいへんカワイイ。

《盆栽藝術家》

　可將任何樹木改變成小人國尺寸的專家。日本因爲人們的住宅都很小，擁有自己庭院的也很少，因此盆栽家們的存在可非常重要。因爲躺在榻榻米上蓋著棉被仰望著盆栽的松樹，也是個享受。此外柑橘的盆栽當然果實味道很差，不能食用，但是花朵卻是非常嬌小可愛。

The Bonsaist

Specialize in producing trees, plants and shrubs in a dwarflike scale. This species is an absolute necessity in a land where city houses are often tiny and rarely have any garden. Because most natives sleep on the floor, it is still possible to look up through the branches of a bonsaied pine tree. Bonsaied orange trees produce astonishingly acerbic fruit but the flowers are cute!

〔キャピキャピやかましい女学生〕

　平日はセーラー服に身を包み、集団で歩き回っている。この人種の男たちよりも背は低いが、横幅の方は負けず劣らず。一方休日になると原宿のような「安全」地域に群がり、アイスクリームをなめながらさらにけたたましい騒音を発する。この種族が作った言語には「バイビー」等あり。

《麻雀般吵鬧的女學生》

　平時穿著一身水手學生服，三五成群。比較起同類的男生們身材略矮，但橫面的體積卻毫不遜色。一到了假日，就成群結隊出現在原宿這種所謂「安全」的地帶，嘴裏舔著冰淇淋，還會發出恐怖的尖叫聲，這種族群甚至創出了自己的語言，包括英文中的「拜拜！」。

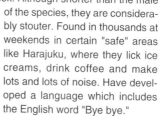

Cackling Schoolgirls

Travel in packs and most wear sailor suits every day of the week. Although shorter than the male of the species, they are considerably stouter. Found in thousands at weekends in certain "safe" areas like Harajuku, where they lick ice creams, drink coffee and make lots and lots of noise. Have developed a language which includes the English word "Bye bye."

〔ＡＶギャル〕

頻繁に衣服を脱ぐのでよく観察できることだが、この人種の体は一部、かすんでボヤケている。たいていはあえぎ声や叫び声くらいで、言語らしきものは発達していない。人前で話す力を得ると深夜テレビに出演し男たちに——いつも野球帽をかぶった映画カントクもその一人——媚を売るようになる。

《 AV 女郎 》

經常在脫衣服，故可以很徹底地觀察。這種族群的身體有部份經常是朦朦朧朧的，語言能力極不發達，大抵只會發出呻吟或尖叫聲。如果有說話的機會，就會常出現在深夜成人電視頻道上，表現出她們的媚功給男人，其中包括一個喜歡戴著棒球帽的某好色電影導演。

The AV Girl

Part of their bodies appear to be of hazy construction, which can be observed when they divest themselves of their plumage—which they do quite often. Most only make throaty noises or emit squeaks. The ones which have learned the power of speech, often appear on late night TV, revealing their charms to a collection of men, one of whom is always wearing a peaked cap!

〔歌舞伎役者〕

熱狂的ファン以外にとっては耐えがたい退屈を与えてくれる役者たちで、全員が男性である。奇妙な声でおそろしくゆっくり話すのも特徴。歌舞伎劇場では英語ばかりか、日本語のイヤホン翻訳サービスまでやっている！人間国宝になる者も多い。全員が男性ということは、この人種は生まれてくるのではなく、どこかで製造されているらしい。

《歌舞伎演員》

除了狂熱的發燒戲迷可免受虐待之外，他們的演出簡直讓人昏昏欲睡、索然無趣，而且演員全屬男性。用奇妙詭異的聲音一字一字念著台詞是其特徵。在歌舞伎劇場中居然還有透過耳機做英日語翻譯的服務呢！而且有不少演員都被列爲人間國寶，這個人種應該不是打娘胎裡出來的，相信是在某地被製造出來的吧？

The Kabuki Actor

Capable of instilling the most indescribable level of boredom in all except the most serious aficionado, these actors are all male and speak a strange language, painfully slowly. In kabuki theaters, an earphone translation service is available in English and in Japanese! A few have been made "Living National Treasures"—until they die. Being all male, it is believed they are created—not born.

〔アイドル〕

やせぎすで幼く、歯並びがひどいのも多い。おしなべて才能はないに等しいが、その金切り声は犬をもたじろがせるのであなどれない。マス・メディアによって大量生産されている彼女たちに歌唱力など必要なく、一夜にして現れては消える生き物である。

《青春偶像》

　　年幼發育尚未完全、齒列不齊者居多。一般説來幾乎沒什麼才能，可是她們獨有高亢尖鋭的聲音足可讓狗兒夾尾竄逃的功力，可不容輕視！靠著媒體得以被大量生產的她們，也不需什麼演唱實力，因為她們屬於一夜之間出現隨即消失的生物。

Miss . . . (Idol)

Excruciatingly thin, incredibly young looking and often equipped with the worst set of teeth you've ever seen, most have virtually no talent. Their voices are so high pitched, dogs wince when they speak. Because this species is spawned by the publicity machine, they need no singing ability and they appear and disappear almost overnight.

〔ザ・ヤクザ〕

　この人種は一見みな同じように見えるが、実は派閥どうしの抗争が激しく、シマをめぐってのいさかいなど日常茶飯事。趣味のよろしい彫り物を肌にほどこし、髪の毛と指の1〜2本は短めが主流。サングラスと金のアクセサリーが好みで言葉づかいの荒っぽいこの人々に接近するのは、やや危険を伴う行為である――特に、「火ィ貸してくれませんか？」なんて言いながら近づくのは。

《大哥》

　這類人種乍看幾乎全都長一個模樣，其實幫派鬥爭相當激烈，常為了地盤火併可說是家常便飯。喜歡在背上紋些其最愛的圖樣，留著短髮及在犯錯時切下手指的是主流。若有戴著墨鏡及全身穿戴金飾並操著一口兄弟語氣的人接近你時，就表示可能會有危險發生，特別是搭訕的語句是「可以借個火嗎？」時。

The Yakuza

Even though they all look the same, this breed is very clannish and often squabble among themselves over territorial matters. Their skins are often gaudily painted, both their hair and at least one little finger are cropped short, they wear dark glasses, gold chains, abuse the language and are very dangerous to approach, especially with phrases like, "Got a light mate!"

〔銀座のホステス〕

　夜行性動物。平日の夕方７時半ごろ新橋・銀座・有楽町の各駅にぞくぞくと現れ、それぞれの小さな巣穴へとかけ込む。客のグラスに水割りを作るためである。髪をきれいにセットし、高価なブランド服か着物に身を包む彼女たちは、めったに「オアソビ」の相手にはなってくれない。みんな夫か恋人、ときにはその両方がいるからだ。深夜１１時半になると、来た時と同じくらい突然に姿を消す。

《銀座媽媽桑》

　夜行性動物。每天一到傍晚７點半左右，她們就會出現在新橋、銀座、有樂町等車站附近，然後再紛紛鑽入各自的小巢穴裏，為來客調製威士忌。梳著漂亮的髮型、身裏高價的名牌服飾或「和服」的媽媽桑們是偶爾能與你出場「伴遊」。通常她們都有丈夫或情人，有的甚至兩者兼備的享齊人之福。一到深夜11點半左右，同來時一樣，她們又會突然消失於人群中。

The Ginza Hostess

Nocturnal, they appear in the hundreds at 7:30 p.m. on week nights at Shinbashi, Ginza and Yurakucho stations and rush off to minute burrows to pour water into their customers' glasses. Always well coiffured and exquisitely dressed in designer clothes or kimono, they are rarely available for "hanky panky" being either married, having boyfriends or both. Disappear as suddenly as they appear at 11:30 p.m.

〔パチンコ店の店長〕

　フォート・ノックス刑務所の看守よりもたくさんのカギ束を腰からぶら下げているゆえ、すぐそれとわかる。また、銀座とタイムズ・スクエアとピカデリー・サーカスが一緒になってかかっても負けそうなほど、彼の巣のネオンはギンギラギンである。昼間はめったに生息地以外へ出歩かないが、夜１１時過ぎには小さなバーなどで見かけられ、小指がないお友達や着物のホステスに囲まれている。無口である。

《柏青「哥」》

　　腰際懸掛著比監獄看守員還多的鑰匙串，所以很容易一眼就認出來。而他們巢穴霓虹燈的輝煌程度毫不遜色於銀座、紐約時報廣場及倫敦的皮卡迪利廣場。這種人通常是白天足不出戶，一過了晚上11點左右即出現在小酒吧裏，身旁圍繞著類似「兄弟」的朋友或是穿著和服的媽媽桑們，本人則沈默寡言。

The Pachinko Manager

Easily distinguished by his carrying more keys than a Fort Knox jailer. His nest has more active neon light than the Ginza, Times Square and Picadilly Circus rolled into one. Rarely seen outside his natural habitat in daylight, but can be found in small night clubs after 11 p.m., usually in the company of members of the pruned pinky set and kimono clad hostesses. Never speaks.

〔（おつむが）超軽量ウオークマン〕

　磁気テープであやつられている原住民。頭から騒音がもれていることが多い。若いうちは原始的部族音楽を好み、年をとるにつれモーツァルトを好む傾向がある。どんよりした目をしていながらも、電車では駅名のアナウンスを聞きのがさないよう注意している。公園ではカップルになったのも見かけられる。——プラグで一つにつながって。

《隨身聽族》

　　一群被錄音磁帶所操控著的原住民。而且大多數會從頭部傾洩出噪音。年輕時偏好原始狂放的族群音樂，一上了年紀則傾向於聆聽莫札特。在電車裏，雖然眼神渙散，但在電車內還是細心聆聽車掌所播報的站名。在公園裡也可看見成雙成對的族群由一條耳機線相牽連著。

The Simple Walkman

Magnetic tape operated native, often with noise emanating from its skull. Young ones produce sounds of tribal music however they often change to Mozart as they age. They maintain glazed eyes, but appear to be tuned to station name announcements when travelling on trains. Occasionally found as couples in parks—plugged together.

〔ファミコン中毒者〕

目はキョロキョロ、指は絶えずせわしなく動いているので、とても見分けやすい。この種の若者はバスや電車で頻繁に見かけられる。一方「ゲーセン」に入りびたるややふけたのは、自動改札機導入により失職した、もと駅の改札係たちである、と言われている。

《超級電玩族》

　　眼神忙亂緊張、手指動個不停，所以非常容易辨認。這種族群的年輕人經常出現於公車或電車上。看他們如此陶醉於「電動玩具中心」及沉迷其中的樣子，有人說那些人就是因爲導入了自動剪票機而慘遭炒魷魚的原車站剪票員。

A Fami-con-aholic

These can be easily discovered because their eyes never stay still and their fingers always fidget. Younger members of this breed can be observed in almost any form of public transport, oblivious to the crowds. It is believed that the older ones who can be found in any "Game Parlor" were once station clippies who have been retired due to the introduction of automatic ticket wickets.

〔親切すぎる宅配員〕

年に2度の贈答シーズンのため繁殖した彼らは、荷物から解放されたい一心でカギのかかっていない所にはどこでも入ってくる。小さなバンには、ギネスブックにも載せきれないほどの配達物を積み込んでいる。ある者は政府との癒着によって一大派閥を成したとか……。

《過度親切的送貨員（不請自進）》

因每年兩次的送禮季節而大量繁殖、也是一種一心想從送貨後得到解放的族群，只要是沒有上鎖的地方就會鑽進來。小小的貨車內裝滿了貨物，幾乎可以名列金氏紀錄。聽說有某位從事這行的人因與政府關係極佳，甚至還發展成一個大財團呢！

Friendly Deliveryman (enters automatically)

Probably created by the biannual, present-giving ritual, this breed will walk into any place unlocked in its efforts to divest itself of its package. Capable of cramming more items into tiny vehicles than the Guinness Book of Records can list. Clans have been formed with some allegedly nefarious government connections.

〔ナイター・ファン〕

ひいきのチームの帽子やシャツを身につけ、ナイター中継があるとテレビに貼り付いてしまう。タバコとビール、さきいかなどの珍味が観戦に必須のアイテム。野球場の入場券が手に入りにくいことからはびこった人種とも言われる。どこかの国の「カウチポテト族」に類似点あり。

《夜間職棒迷》

穿著自己「死忠」擁護的球隊衣帽，一有夜間實況轉播即黏在電視機前面。香煙、啤酒及魷魚絲等零嘴是觀戰時的必需品。有人說這些人是因為球賽入場券難以到手才繁殖出來的。這和某國的「洋芋片族」文化似乎頗有異曲同工之妙哩！

The "Naitā" (Night Baseball) Fan

Dressed in the plumage of his favourite team, this species becomes glued to the television set while armed with two packs of cigarettes, a case of beer and assorted packs of shredded dried fish, or other strange snacks. Spawned by the fact, baseball game tickets sell out within minutes of being put on sale. Similar to other nation's "Couch Potatoes."

〔深夜通勤族〕

　この生物には、つり革にぶら下がって眠れる特性がある。男も女もいれば、会社員から学生までと層も厚い。座っている場合、二人連れであれば互いの肩にもたれ合って眠る。だが連れがいなくとも、他人の肩を無断借用して、やはり眠るのである。彼らには第六感が備わっているらしく、自分の降りる駅でぱっと目を覚ます。忘れ物も得意で、カサや書類かばん、中にはクツまで忘れる者がいる。

《深夜通勤族》

　這種生物的特性就是懸掛在電車的吊環下睡覺。有男有女，從上班族到學生，涵蓋層面相當廣。當坐著時，兩人互倚同伴的肩而睡，若沒有同伴時，也會擅自借用他人的肩膀進入夢鄉。他們有著與生俱來的第六感，總會在該下的車站前自動醒來，不過，遺忘物品也是他們的專長，從雨傘到書本，甚至連鞋都還有人會忘記哩。

The Late Night Commuter

This breed can strap-hang and sleep at the same time. Both male and female, the species vary from office workers to students. Seated, if in a pair, they will sleep on each other's shoulders; if alone they will sleep on other's shoulders. They appear to have an inbred sixth sense which switches their eyes on precisely as they reach their home station. Often forget umbrellas, briefcases and sometimes their shoes.

〔魚屋のオヤジ〕

　つるつる頭にうっすらと無精ヒゲ、という手合いがなぜか多い。誰も通りかからなくても大声で呼び込みを続ける奇癖があるため、魚に話しかけているのではないか、と誤解されがち。毎日午前3時に築地へ群れ集まり、マグロの値段をせり合っている。

《魚店的老爹》

　　不曉得是何道理，這種人通常是頭頂光禿、不修邊幅，也不管有沒有人經過，總是具備喜歡扯開嗓門大聲叫賣的怪癖，所以常被誤爲是在和魚講話。每天清晨3點就群聚在中央魚市場，競相標購鮪魚是他們的例行工作。

The Fishmonger

Never seem to have any hair but nearly all need a shave. They are always loudly calling their wares, even if nobody is around. This has led to a mistaken belief that they talk to the fish. Can be discovered in their multitudes at Tsukiji market at 3 a.m. squabbling over the price of tuna.

〔ディズニーランダー〕

　老いを知らない。毎日、儀式のごとく何万人となって開園時間きっかりに集まり、数分間の興奮のために一日中でも行列をつくるのである。しかるのち、広大な敷地のはるか彼方に見える次のアトラクションへと移動する——群れをなして。彼らの部族衣装は、ミッキーマウスのお耳やドナルドのくちばし付き帽子など多様。もちろん「お名前刺しゅうサービス」付きの代物である。

《狄斯奈樂園迷》

　　不服老。就像參加某種慶典一般，每天隨著數萬人集結在樂園門口等開門。爲了數分鐘的興奮而排一整天的隊也不以爲苦。過不了多久，就看到他們又成群在廣大的園地中，朝下一個目標前進。這個族群的服裝特色是戴著有米老鼠耳朵或唐老鴨嘴巴的帽子等，當然帽上還繡著免費贈送的英文名字。

The Disneylander

Ageless, these are participants in a daily ritual gathering, where hundreds of thousands of them will arrive at exactly the same time, queue all day for a few minutes of excitement and then all depart for the far corners of the land—together. All wear some form of tribal costume varying from Mickey Mouse ears to caps with Donald Duck beaks, many with their names—in English, embroidered on them.

〔エレベーターガール〕

非の打ちどころのない制服を着用し、マニキュアもヘアスタイルもバッチリ。ボタンを押し、床を見つめ、乗降客におじぎをし、各階の売り場案内を復唱するだけの日々である。彼女たちはたいへんきれいな日本語を使うため、外国人でも聞き取りやすいほど。しかし英語の方は……。

《電梯女郎》

　　穿著光鮮帥氣的制服，不管是指甲或髮型都完美無瑕。按著鈕、眼睛注視著樓板、對乘客鞠躬行禮、反覆介紹各樓層的特色，週而復始。她們操著一口漂亮的日語，連外國人也很容易聽懂，不過英文方面可就... ...。

The Elevator Operator

Always in impeccable uniform, perfectly manicured with neat hairstyles, they spend their lives, pushing buttons, looking at the ground, bowing people in and out of the doors and reciting excitedly about the goodies on every floor. They use such a level of polite Japanese, many foreigners can understand them, even though most don't know one single word of English.

〔電話ボックスの広告シール〕

　歓楽街のあらゆる電話ボックスに無数にばらまかれ、年齢に関係なく男性諸氏の視線をくぎづけにする。コピーは扇情的だが、実体はひどく期待はずれなのがほとんど。中には、写真の女性が１５年間変わらないのもある！これを収集したい向きにひとこと。このシールの接着力は非常に強力なので、２枚一組にして貼り合わせておくとグッド。

《電話亭中的小貼紙》

　歡樂街上所有的電話亭幾乎全貼滿了這種廣告，並且吸引各種年齡層男性的視線。廣告很煽情，但大多與實際大有差距。其中有些照片裏的女郎甚至十五年來如一日。因爲它們背後的黏膠實在太強了，如果你有興趣收集，建議你兩張背對背黏成一組，good！

The Telephone Booth Stickers

Found in their hundreds in all entertainment districts, these are eagerly sought after by hawks of all ages. Often offering wildly exciting themes, they can also be quite disappointing. Some have featured the same chick on it for the last fifteen years! If you plan to collect some, please stick them back-to-back because the glue will not come off anything it adheres to!

23

〔コンドームの訪問販売員〕

どんな時にも生き残ってきた、しぶといおばさんたち。昨今はエイズのため、セールストークも一層説得力を増した。しかし、玄関に出迎えたのがガイジン、それも半裸だったりすると、なぜか沈黙してしまう。自動販売機が普及したので、この種は絶滅の途をたどっているのかもしれない。

《保險套推銷員》

　　無論什麼時代都會想盡辦法存活下來的頑強老婆婆們。最近因爲愛滋病，她們推銷時的功力也大爲增進。可是當前來應門的是一個半裸的老外時，不知怎麼卻啞口無語。由於自動販賣機的普及，這種族群遲早會走上絕種之途吧。

The Door-to-door Condom Saleswoman

Incredibly tenacious, they have always been a part of the scenery, however since the advent of AIDS they have additional things to say. Apparently become speechless if the person opening the door happens to be a foreigner—particularly if a partially clothed male. This breed may be dying out due to the increase in vending machines for their products.

〔ＰＴＡ会長〕

決まって女性である。その育ちのよさ（すなわち夫の職業のこと）によって、他の父母たちより上の地位についた。校長たちにとって脅威の存在であるばかりか、父母たちにも信じがたいことをやらせてしまう——例えば５００人分のおにぎりや弁当を作るとか。金歯は３本くらいあるのがふつうで、身に着けるのは高そうな宝石類とオーダーメイドのスーツ。もちろん大の嫌煙家である。

《ＰＴＡ會長（家長會會長）》

絕對是女性。由於她們身出名門（亦即先生的職業），使得她們的地位凌駕在其他家長之上。她們的存在有時候對校長來說是一種威脅，甚至還會叫其他家長們做些令人難以想像的事，譬如做五百人份的壽司或便當。這種人一般裝著３顆金牙，身上穿著訂做的名牌套裝、戴著極爲昂貴的珠寶，當然她們對反對吸煙方面的貢獻，也是不遺餘力。

The PTA President

Always female, whose breeding (i.e. her husband's job) carries her above the status of the lesser parents. Have been known to create fear in school principals and make parents do amazing things like produce rice balls or lunch boxes for 500. Often have at least three gold teeth, usually wear fabulously expensive jewelry, tailored suits and never smoke.

〔お役所の公務員〕

官庁や市・区役所に生息する。この人種は基本的に、2つに大別できる——親切なのと、底意地悪いくらい不親切なのに。弁解にはたけているが、その他に関してはおしなべて口下手。両腕の黒い腕貫とゴムの指サックがトレードマーク。手続きのしかたがよくわからない人々と申請書に記入ミスをした人を徹底的に苦しめることで有名。

《基層公務員》

　　棲息在公家機關或鄉區公所。這種人基本上可分爲：對人親切與極度怠慢不親切的兩類。在辯解時滔滔不絕，但除此之外毫無能力可言，且口才平平。兩手臂套著黑色護套及手指頭上戴著橡膠指套是其註冊商標。此外讓那些不懂得如何辦手續或填錯申請表格的人徹底吃足苦頭，是他們最出名的地方。

The Civil Servant

Found in all government buildings and city authority offices. Basically of two types, helpful or decidedly unhelpful. All are masters of defensive speech, but often difficult to make speak at all. Usually seen wearing black plastic sleeve covers with two or more rubber tipped fingers. Will prey on the uninformed and those who have filled out the wrong forms.

〔新人類〕

他の日本人のような無個性な服装はせず、むろんネクタイを嫌う。男も女も同じように見えるこの人種は、独自のコミュニケーション手段を使うので、旧人類には全く理解できない。しょっちゅう文句をこぼし、そんな時だけは他人に意志を伝えられるのだから理不尽。

《新人類》

　　穿著上絕對不會穿像其他日本人般的那樣沒有個性，當然也最厭惡領帶。這群看起來似男非女的人類的溝通方式非常獨特，舊人類是完全無法理解的。整天只會抱怨個沒完，因為只有在這個時候才能正確傳遞其意，所以常也都是些歪理。

The New Generation

A new breed who have dropped the dull garb of the rest of the species and don't even wear ties. Often both sexes look identical, and they have even developed a new form of communication pattern to prevent the older generation from understanding what they are doing. The only time they are intelligible is when they are complaining about something, which they do most of the time.

〔正座〕

体格や性別、年齢にかかわらず、この国の人々は生まれた時からこの座り方を練習している。年配女性ともなると、朝から晩までこのまま座っていられる。もしガイジンが3分以上正座をしたならば、その後何日かは拷問のような痛みが足に残るだろう。しかし、日本人は感情を顔に表さないことでも有名である。臨床的見地から考えると、彼らもやはり苦痛を感じているのかもしれない。研究課題である。

《正坐》

　　不分體格、性別或年齡，這國的人民從小即被訓練學習「正坐」。上了年紀的女性更是有辦法從早坐到晚。如果叫一個老外坐3分鐘以上，相信那種如受酷刑的痛楚不知會延續幾天呢。日本人一向以不輕易的將感情表露於表情中而聞名，可是就臨床上來看，他們應該還是會感到痛苦才對，這方面是個值得研究的好題目。

The Traditional Squat

Performed from birth, this method of sitting is practiced by the whole species, irrespective of size, sex or age. Aged women can retain this position all day. Foreigners cannot execute this pose for more than a few minutes without experiencing excruciating pain in their legs for days afterward. The Japanese however, have mastered the art of keeping a straight face. Clinically observed, they may be suffering. Research continues!

〔パンク〕

　以前は日本に存在しないと言われていたが、最近になって日曜の代々木公園あたりに出没する人種である。同公園の音楽に誘われて出てくるようだが、実は耳が遠いようでもある。外国のパンク野郎と見かけは変わらないものの、こちらは声にハクがなく、態度も従順。とはいえ、やたら近寄らないのが賢明だ。

《龐克族》

　　以前日本是沒有這種族群的，不過最近一到假日卻經常出現在代代木公園附近。他們似乎是被公園裏的音樂給吸引過來，其實他們重聽的程度還相當厲害呢，外表看起來與外國龐克族沒什麼兩樣，其實他們不像外國人那麼威風凜凜，態度也比較順從，不過沒事的時候，還是不要隨便靠近。

The Punk

Once believed non-existent in Japan, this species has recently surfaced in areas like Tokyo's Yoyogi Park on Sundays. They appear to be attracted by the music in the park and also appear to be quite deaf. Although they look similar to punks of other lands, this species often talks in high-pitched voices and is usually docile—still, best avoided.

〔観光ガイド〕

目の覚めるような色の制服で手には旗を持ち、観光客をゾロゾロ引き連れていたり、観光バスの入口で待ち受けている。自分の背後の風景を透視できるだけでなく、誰も聞いていなくてもしゃべり続ける能力がある。アンプの力を借りれば、静まりかえった寺に眠る死者をも起こすという。いつも石鹸の匂いがする。

《導遊小姐》

　　身著色彩醒目的制服，手持旗子，後頭拖著一群觀光客，在遊覽車門口前待命。不僅能透視自己身後的風景，還具有雖沒人聆聽但還能滔滔不絕說個沒完的能力。據說透過擴音器的幫助，連靜靜躺在寺院裏的先人都會被她們吵醒，而且身上還總是飄著一股清香的肥皂味兒。

The Tour Guide

Brightly colored plumage with hat and flag, there is one in front of every crowd and at the door of every tour bus. They can apparently see through the back of their heads and have learned how to talk continuously even if nobody is listening and when armed with electronic amplification can rouse the dead at any serene temple or shrine. Always smell of soap.

〔歌舞伎町のホステス〕

　銀座のホステスと同じく夜行性ながら、はるかによくしゃべり、よく飲む。衣装は派手なのも地味なのもいるが、いずれにせよカンタンに脱いでしまうという。客のニーズで出前もするのか、まだ早い時間に徘徊していることも。英語を話す者も少なくない。注意すべきは、指の短いパトロン付きが多い点。

《新宿歌舞伎町的女侍》

　　同銀座的媽媽桑一樣屬於夜行性動物，但比較起來她們更多話、酒量更好。有的打扮入時、有的則不然，不管是那一種類型，會率性的就脫掉衣物為其特徵。有時為了客人的需要，他們也有電話外送的服務，時間還早的時候就四處遊蕩。會講英語的人還不少，不過值得注意的是，在她們周遭通常有「兄弟」隨時照應，要小心為是。

The Kabukicho Hostess

Similar to the Ginza breed, also nocturnal, but talk more and drink real liquor. Plumage is either gaudy or very simple, but always easy to remove. Often can cater to other needs of their customers, are sometimes seen prowling in the early hours and many can speak English. Beware, most have short-fingered patrons.

〔駅の改札係〕

原始的な宗教舞踊に似た音楽をその脳裏で奏でながら、休みなく神経質にハサミを鳴らす人種。ハサミの使いすぎによるパンチドランカーで、人の顔すらろくに見ていない。なのにキセルは瞬時に見分けられるのだから、タダモノではない。自動改札機が普及する昨今、地方へと大移動しているようである。

《車站剪票員》

通常腦中一邊響著類似原始宗教般的舞蹈音樂，有點神經質似的手指一邊不停地動著剪刀發出旋律。由於剪票過多所帶來的「剪票職業病」，有時連他人的臉孔也不正眼看一下，但是有人想蹺票時，卻可以馬上發現，這時才發現他們不是機器。在自動剪票機普及的今日，聽說已經開始大移動，已經移到鄉下地方去了。

The Ticket Puncher

Restless, nervous, forever clicking to some unheard melody in its head with a rhythm akin to some ancient cult dance, this species is dying out. Punch drunk to the point of never looking at faces, it can spot an underpaid fare in a flash. As automatic ticket wickets take over in the cities, they are all migrating to the countryside.

〔化石人間〕

　身長は１５０センチ以下。大のガイジン嫌いだが、この人種はしょせん誰もかれも嫌いらしい。どんな時もニコリともしないのがその証拠。ショウノウ臭いことから、実は彼らは昔々何か大罪を犯したサムライで、罪ほろぼしのためにあの世へ成仏できないのだ、と学者たちは言っている。

《化石人類》

　　身高在150公分以下。最討厭高大魁梧的「老外」，這種人種基本上也厭惡其他人類，臉上從不露出笑容爲其證據，身上常帶著一股樟腦味，因此有些學者說，他們本是犯下大錯的武士，爲了贖罪，因此還在世間尚未成佛。

The Dinosaur

Never grow taller than 5 feet and appear to hate foreigners, it is believed that this species hates everyone because there is never any smile to be seen.

Because they smell of moth balls, anthropologists conclude that they are in fact ancient samurai, who have committed some awful crime against the Gods and have been left on Earth to atone.

〔セクシーボーイ〕

　肉体的には外国の同類と共通点はあるが、こちらの方はムキムキゴリラではない。日中は公園などでシェイプアップに励み、夜になるとホストクラブで金満オバさまの相手になったりする。危険性はなく、男性客からも女性客からも「カワイーイ！」と言われてしまう。

《日本舞男》

　除了身體與外國同類者有許多共通之處外，日本的不像國外那般如粗線條的「猩猩」般。平常白天在公園等地不斷鍛鍊身體，一到夜晚即到牛郎倶樂部與渾身「金」味的老女人為伍。不具危險性，有時男客人或女客人都會誇獎他「好可愛！」。

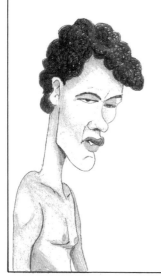

The Stud

Although similar in build to foreign species, these are not your usual hulk. During daylight may be observed in parks doing ritual exercises, but at night are mostly to be discovered in Host Bars with middle aged, rich, female patrons. Not at all threatening and to most visitors of both sex, they look "cute"!

34

〔中年お嬢様〕
　常に冷静で孤高を保ち、たまに付き合う友達と言ったら鼻も
ちならないテングばかり。ふだんは人形のようにすかしてい
る。話しかけられれば作り笑いを浮かべるが、ろくに答えもし
ない。一生独身主義、でなければすでに出戻りというのが多
い。いったい何か仕事しているのかどうか、よくわからない
人種である。

《中年小姐》

　　始終保持著冷靜孤傲，偶爾與朋友聚在一起也是自負得不得了。平常像
洋娃娃一樣地好哄，一與她攀談臉上即勉強堆出笑容，但卻不多做回答。一
輩子抱著獨身主義，要不然就是已經「回門」，也不知道是從事何種職業，
是一種難以理解的人種。

Ojō-san

Cool, this breed is either alone or found
in identical groups who all maintain a
very high opinion of themselves. Doll-
like in their own minds, if spoken to, will
force a smile, but usually will not make
any reply. Always turn out to be somebody's aunt, never marry, or are already divorced. It is unknown if they
actually work.

〔証券マン〕

景気の良し悪しにかかわらず、表情を変えない人々。２４時間働いているようだが、ときどき早朝の始発電車や深夜のラーメン屋で見かけられる。他の国の同業者のようなリッチぶりにはとても及ばないが、暮らし向きは悪くなく、ほとんどが既婚者である。

《證券從業人員》

這群人不論景氣好壞與否，表情始終如一。每天彷彿 24 小時奉獻於工作中，偶爾會出現在早班的電車裏或深夜的麵攤上。雖不及其他國家同業們那般的富裕，但生活上倒不虞匱乏，大多數都已婚。

The Stockbroker

Boom or bust this breed never changes expression. They appear to work all day and night, however a few can be spotted in early morning trains going home or around midnight in all-night noodle stalls. Nowhere near as wealthy as their foreign counterparts, they do however exude the air of comfortableness and are all married.

〔碁の名人〕

　１９の１９乗通りもの順列をあやつるゲームの達人たる者、何時間ものあいだ食事もせずものも言わず、微動だにせず座っていられるのである。碁盤に打たれる石の音が、彼の耳には音楽となる。国際電話の９ケタの番号など、即座に暗記できてしまうのだ。

《圍棋老仙》

　　精於操控 19 乘 19 行列遊戲的專家，可以不食不言，動也不動地坐上數個鐘頭。棋子下在棋盤上的聲音聽在他們耳裏無異是種音樂。就連九位數的國際直撥電話的號碼，他們也能當場一字不差地背下來。

The Igo Master

This master of a game with 19^{19} possible permutations, is capable of sitting almost motionless for hours, without food and without saying anything. The click of the stones on the thick wooden board is music to his ears. It is believed masters can recall any one of 123,456,789 international, direct dial telephone numbers—instantly.

〔極左 / 極右〕

　改造された装甲車に乗り、拡声器で我慢できない騒音を流す男たちのこと。同じ日本人でさえ、彼らが何を言っているのかよくわからないと言う。ふだんはどこかにひそんでいるが、外国のＶＩＰが来日するたびに、やたらと活動的になる。自分たちよりはるかに多い警官たちに囲まれると従順になるが、やかましさは変わらない。

《極左/極右派》

　一群坐著改裝過的戰車，用擴音器播放著令人無法忍受的噪音的一群無聊男子。連日本人也人聽不懂他們在講什麼。平常的日子不知躲在何處，每到有貴賓來訪時，便會積極的活動起來，當自己的人比警察少又被警察團團圍住時，則顯得很順從，但吵鬧的特性絲毫不會收斂。

The Ultra Left/Right

Mostly male hawks, this breed travels about in re-conditioned riot police buses, equipped with loudspeakers whose level is set a few decibels above the threshold of pain. Unintelligible—even to the natives. Usually in hiding, but become very active whenever there are visiting VIPs from overseas. Will form long, noisy but very orderly rallies, where they are usually surrounded by a police force outnumbering them ten to one.

〔政治家〕
　この手の人間は男女とも毎年ある時期に現れて明け方から深夜まで少なくとも2個以上の拡声器を積んだ車で住宅街を走り回っては白手袋で手を振り金切り声の女に自分の名前を何度も連呼させるのである。車を止めれば子供たちにキスもする！

《政治家》

　這種族群不論男女每年到某一定時期時，即從黎明出現到深夜，並在車上最少裝著兩個以上的擴音器不停巡迴在大街小巷。並由女生揮著帶著白手套的手，反覆不停的以尖銳的語調呼喊出自己的大名。有時甚至會停下車來親吻小孩哩！

The Politician

Both the male and the female of this species appear at certain times of the year and employ a shrill female voice which they use to repeat their own names over and over again while touring the suburbs from dawn to dusk in vehicles with at least two loudspeakers on the roof and about six pairs of white gloved hands waving from the windows. Kiss children if stopped!

〔あまり害のない酔っぱらい〕

深夜の電車には必ず1人か2人いる。ある傾斜角度で眠りに落ち、そのまま座席にズルズルと倒れこむという芸当ができる。深夜通勤族と同様、自分の降りる駅で起きられる第六感を備えている。そうでない者は、終点で親切な駅員さんによって運び出されることになる。

《無害醉貓》

深夜電車裏一定會有一、二位。以某個傾斜角度沈沈入睡，並且還有順著這個姿勢，滑躺到椅子上的絕活。與深夜通勤族般，具有某種第六感，一到了自己欲下車的車站，就會霎然醒了過來。此外的醉貓，則由親切的車站職員，一一的將他們抬出去。

The Lesser Obnoxious Drunk

Found in ones and twos on most late night transport, this breed has developed the ability to go to sleep at an angle, and then fall sideways onto the seat. Most are equipped with the same sixth sense as the late night commuter in being able to sense their home station. Those who don't, are eased off the train at the terminus by the vigilant station staff.

〔たいへん害のある酔っぱらい〕

この連中とは決してかかわり合わない事。強烈なニオイをまき散らし、何でもないことに腹を立て、吐くわめくわで手に負えない。連れのいない場合が多いので、若い女の子にしつこくからむか、でなければ都合よく居合わせたガイジンに日本語のレッスンを始める。どちらにせよ大変やっかいである。アドバイス：車輌をかえること。

《有害醉鬼》

　與這些人最好不要有任何牽扯。他們散發著強烈的酒臭味，對任何芝麻小事都會藉題發作，又吐又鬧令人束手無策。通常都沒有人相伴，因此不是緊緊的糾纏年輕女孩，要不然就是趁機對鄰座的外國人開始教授日語課程，兩者都令人頭痛。建議：改搭別輛車。

The Greater Obnoxious Drunk

This breed should be avoided at all costs. Surrounded by a pungent aroma, they are quick to take umbrage at nothing, often throw up and are normally very noisy. Usually alone, they will make a beeline for young girls on a train or try their best to teach any handy foreigner the Japanese language, by shouting at him or her. Advice: Change carriages.

〔カラオケ・ファン〕

　男女を問わずこのカラオケ鳥たちは、はるか彼方にいてもやかましくてそれとわかってしまう。アンプの力を借りても、調子っぱずれは治るものではない。デュエットやトリオになると、そのうるささはガマンの限界を超える。騒音に鈍感な者どうしで仲間を作っている。残念ながら彼らは当分絶滅しそうにないどころか、海辺や公園、果ては海外へも生息分布を広げてしまった。

《卡拉 OK 愛好家》

　　即使在遙遠的另一方也能聽到這些卡拉 OK 鳥們不分男女的吵鬧聲，馬上便知道是怎麼回事兒。儘管有擴音器的輔助，但那荒腔走板的歌聲往往還是沒有藥救。若是遇到男女對唱或三重唱的歌曲，其吵鬧聲更是令人無法忍受，通常只有對噪音鈍感的人才會與那種人為伍。遺憾的是，他們尚未有絕種的傾向，反而是生生不息地遍佈海邊、公園等地，甚至連海外也有他們的蹤跡哩。

The Ruby-throated Karaoke Singer

The songbirds of the species, of both sexes, these can be heard long before they are seen. They are electronicly amplified, but unable to carry a tune and the sound becomes louder and more intolerable when "singing" as a duet or trio. Gather together in small flocks who are oblivious to the noise. Unfortunately, not under immediate threat of extinction and can sometimes be seen on beaches, in parks and even foreign countries.

〔女子プロレスラー〕

象みたいなのからアリんこまでサイズはさまざまで、容姿も
カワイイのもいればシャレにならないほどひどいのもおり、
極端である。可愛い方が意地悪で、ブスの方がけなげだった
りする。引退後は「タレント」となる場合が多いが、それはつ
まり歌も演技もできないという意味である。

《女子職業摔角手》

從大象體態到螞蟻體型各種尺寸應有盡有，容貌方面也有「可愛型」和
不怎麼上相的「UG型」，相當極端。可愛的那一型通常心眼不太好，而「
UG型」的就比較開朗且有英雄氣概。這種人退休後大多會成為螢幕上的特別
來賓，當然這是說在歌唱及演技方面，都比人略遜一籌的意思。

Female Wrestlers

Varying in size from elephantine to the
GoodYear blimp, some are fairly attractive
while others are absolutely, horrendously
ugly. The former are usually nasty, while
the latter are often quite sweet. After giving
up the wrestling ring
will quite often become
"talent" singers—meaning
they can't sing or act.

〔ハネムーナー〕

　ハワイやサンフランシスコ、シドニー、グアム、サイパンへと、子作りの儀式に旅立つべく空港にあふれかえる新婚カップルたちのこと。一目でそれとわかる服装で、日焼けも控えめに帰国する――親戚や知人に配る２００個以上のお土産と、何枚もの写真をたずさえて。そしてその写真は後日、なぜ新居を買えなかったかの理由の一つとして役立つのである。

《蜜月佳偶》

　　在機場到處可見到這種人，一群急忙飛往夏威夷、舊金山、雪梨、關島、塞班島等舉行製造孩子儀式的新婚夫婦。從他們的服裝上一眼就可認出來，也不想多曬些陽光就帶著超過兩百份以上的土產(Omiyage)及數千張照片回國，這些要給親朋好友的禮物及那疊可觀的照片正好說明了為何沒辦法購買新居的理由。

The Honeymooners

Swarm in pairs at airports migrating to the ritual breeding grounds of Hawaii, San Francisco, Sydney, Guam and Saipan. Always return in identical plumage without suntans, but with thousands of photographs so they can remember why they cannot afford to buy a nest, as well as at least two hundred packs of presents, one for every single person whom they know.

〔相撲とり〕

この国の在来種であり、どこか神格化されている存在。この宗教儀式めいた舞踊について、他のどんなダンスをもしのぐ数の出版物が出ている。信じられないほどよく食べる。なぜか結婚相手はとても小柄な女性が多く、その結果生まれてくるのは平均サイズの子供たち。しかしいったいどうやって作ったのか、知る由もない。

《相撲》

属於此國的原有品種，某部份有點被神格化。市售有關這種類似宗教儀式舞蹈書籍的數量遠遠超過其他類的出版品。而其食量大得驚人，不知什麼原因他們的結婚對象卻又極為嬌小，因此生出來的小孩，都是平均的尺寸。但是怎麼製造出這些孩子那就不得而知了。

Sumō-tori

A classic of the species, considered by all in the flock to be some form of deity, they perform a ritual dance, which has had more written about it than any other dance on earth. Eat the most amazing amount of seed. When marry, tend to attract tiny females and produce normal-sized offspring. It is unknown how they mate.

〔真夜中のレンタルビデオ店の店員〕

オソロシげな風貌の者が多いが、実は柔和な人柄で、肌もひよわに青白い。まちがって別のテープを貸し出しケースに入れてしまうのはお手のものだが、洋画の原題はよく読めないのでカタカナに頼りがち。おかげでLやVの入っている題名の洋画ビデオを彼らに探してもらうのは、至難のワザなのである。

唯一

《深夜錄影帶店店員》

多爲外貌猙獰，但實際卻個性溫和、有點虛弱且臉色蒼白的男孩。常把其他的錄影帶裝錯到外帶的盒子內，因爲不懂洋片的英文名稱，因此非常依賴片假名的注音。也因此拜託他們幫忙找片名含有 L 和 V 的洋片錄影帶是非常困難的事情。

Late Night Video Rental Clerk

Although often exceedingly ferocious looking, they are invariably mild and very pale colored. Adroit at putting the wrong video into a carrying box, they are usually quite incapable of actually pronouncing the English titles on the tapes, relying on the *katakana* version. This makes it almost impossible to order any film which contains an L or a V in the title.

〔真夜中のレンタルビデオ店の客〕

　やっとの思いで借り出したビデオをしっかと胸に抱き、コソコソと伏し目がちに、しかし物凄いスピードで家路を急ぐ。たいがい一人で店にやってきて、秘密めいた奥の一角に隠れるように入っていく。ぜったい店員と視線を合わせず、ケースの中身も確認しないで料金を払って出ていってしまう。

《深夜借錄影帶的客人》

　　這些人常如釋重負般，胸前緊抱著租來的錄影帶，偷偷摸摸的低著頭，衝向回家的路上。大多是單獨一個人到出租店前，鑽入店裡後立即躲進隱密的角落。出店門時，視線絕不和店員相對，也不看看盒子內是否裝錯，便立刻付錢離開。

Late Night Video Renter

Furtive, this species can often be seen, scurrying home with their spoils clutched tightly to their chests, eyes downcast. Usually lone shoppers, they skulk about the concealed part of the video store, never look at the clerk and pay for their merchandise without checking the contents of the pack.

〔女子社会人バレーボールのエース〕

電話をとること以外の事務は全くできないものの、企業イメージ向上のために有用とされている。足が長すぎて日本の事務机には座ることができず、またバレーの試合をしばらく休むと、猫背が直らなくなってしまう。30歳前後で姿を消していく人たち。

《公司隊的女排球明星》

　　這種人除了接聽電話以外，完全不懂公司事務，只被用於提高企業形象。由於腿太長，無法使用日本尺寸的辦公桌，此外一段時間未參加排球比賽後，就變得駝背而一副無精打采的樣子。約 30 歲左右便會從公司消失。

The Company Volleyball Star

Absolutely incapable of doing any office work other than answering the telephone, this breed is reserved for corporate image enhancement. Far too tall to sit with its legs under the average Japanese table, they develop a permanent stoop if left off the volleyball pitch for too long. Seem to disappear around the age of 30.

〔近所の「人間フライデー」〕

　異常に発達した聴覚があり、80メートル向こうでこぼれ落ちたウワサ話を、10秒後には近所中に言いふらしてしまう。新聞がなかった時代には、日本唯一のマスコミ機関であった。彼女たちの亭主は風采のあがらないタイプで、家事ばかりか編み物までやってしまう男も少なくない。

《鄰居的長舌婦》

　聽覺異常發達，能在十秒鐘後，把80公尺外聽來的小道謠言傳遍附近鄰人。在沒有報紙的時代，是日本唯一的報導機構。她們的丈夫多爲其貌不揚、只做家事，甚至打毛線的男人。

The Neighborhood Gossip Monger

Appear to be equipped with the most acute sense of hearing, this breed can hear a rumor drop at 80 meters (50 yards) and can pass a message around a district in 10 seconds. Prior to the advent of newspapers, they were the only form of mass communication in Japan. Always married to diminutive husbands who do the housework, some of whom can actually knit.

〔主婦〕

短期滞在のガイジンには視野に入らない存在。しかしこのメンドリたちの権力は絶大で、巣の中をとりしきり、ヒヨコらの教育やエサはもちろん、財布まで管理している場合が多い。オンドリを尻に敷いている割りには、彼らの帰宅が遅いのにはあまり文句を言わない。エプロン姿の彼女たちは、近所の買い物と地元のお祭り以外、めったに巣から離れようとしない。

《家庭主婦》

短期居留的外國人看不到她們的存在。這種「母鳥」的權力非常大，負責家中各種事情，除了「小鳥」的教育和餵食，往往也掌控家庭的財政支出。雖然對「公鳥」擁有絕對的發言權，但卻不太抱怨他們下班遲歸的事。穿著圍裙的她們除了到附近買東西和參加當地慶典，很少會輕易的離開她們的「巢」。

The Housewife

Often quite invisible to visiting foreigners, this hen rules the roost in most nests, often controlling the purse, always controlling the education and feeding of the chicks and quite oblivious to the late arrival home of the roster although she sometimes hen-pecks. Often wear an apron and rarely are seen far from the nest except at neighborhood shops or local festivals.

〔寿司職人〕

決して口をきかない。白衣をまとい、外科医にも劣らぬ清潔な手をしている。巨大なメスを振りかざし、透けるほどの薄さに魚を切ってみせる。寿司めしを四角ににぎってさまざまな魚の小片をのせ、彼らの芸術は完成する。海外のヘルシーフード偏執狂たちの崇拝の対象でもある。

《壽司師傅》

　　從不開口說話，穿著潔白的衣服，雙手乾淨的程度不會輸給外科醫師，揮舞著巨大的「手術刀」，表演著把魚切成可以透視般的薄片的功夫，並把壽司米捏成四角形，再放上各種生魚片，便完成他們的「藝術品」。他們也成為國際健康食品「偏執狂」人士崇拜的對象。

The Sushiya

Never speak. They are dressed in hospital white and bear hands as scrupulously clean as any surgeon. Can wield a scalpel of monstrous size and slice through raw fish so thinly the result is transparent. Construct works of art with bits of assorted seafood atop hand shaped vinegared rice blocks. This breed is highly sought after among foreign health food fanatics.

〔受付嬢〕

　日本中どんな所に行っても、最初と最後に必ず出くわす女性たちのこと。企業の制服に身を包む彼女たちは、背すじを伸ばして座り続けることと方向を指すことの専門職である。美しくマニキュアをほどこしたそのツメがあまりに長いので、タイプはもちろん打てないし、プッシュホンすら鉛筆の頭を使わざるをえない。

《櫃台接待小姐》

　　不論到日本任何地方，進入拜訪和告辭時必然會碰到的女性族群。她們穿著企業制服，主要的工作是專門負責挺直腰桿長時間坐著並負責指示方向。由於精心修剪的指甲太長，除了無法打字之外，只能靠鉛筆的筆頭撥按鍵電話。

The Receptionist

The first and last thing you see when entering or leaving any place in Japan. Usually wearing some type of corporate plumage, this species specializes in sitting bold upright and pointing the way. They bear beautifully manicured claws, far too long to allow them to type and operate push button telephones with pencil ends.

〔かわいげのないガキ〕

欧米のテレビ番組などの悪影響でこういうガキどもが増えたという人もいるが、このタイプは昔からいたのである。金持ちの実力者が父親である場合が多い。当然ブランドものしか着ず、それもブランド名がよく見えるように着るところが、実にカワイクない。

《令人氣結的小鬼》

雖然有人歸罪這是受了歐美電視節目的影響，這種小鬼才增加的，但應該早在從前便有這種族群。往往有個有錢有勢的父親，只穿名牌衣物，但仍常把品牌標誌顯露在別人能夠看得到的地方，事實上是不太可愛。

The Spoilt Brat

Some people believe this species of chick came about due to the influence of foreign television, however research has proved they have always been in existence. Most often, turn out to be the offspring of the only person in Japan whom you have to respect and be nice to. Their clothing is always designer brand and worn so that the label is visible.

〔ロッカー〕

ブカブカか、でなければピッタリ体にはりつくような、悪趣味で極彩色の服を好む。外国のミュージシャンの真似が多く、中には本人たちよりうまいのもいる。日曜日の代々木公園にたくさん現れ、耳をつんざく大音響で演奏して少年少女を狂喜させている。

《搖滾迷》

　　不是穿著鬆垮垮的特大號，就是偏好穿五顏六色的緊身衣褲，沒有搭配服飾的眼光。多數是模仿外國歌手，但其中也不乏唱得比原唱者更好的。每到星期天就會聚集在東京澀谷的代代木公園，以震耳欲聾的音量來演奏，常讓圍觀的「弟妹」們興奮異常。

The Rock Star

Outrageous, multicolored plumage and clothing which is either four sizes too large or exceedingly tight. Imitate other nations' songbirds—sometimes better than the original sounds. Gather in their multitudes in places like the east edge of Yoyogi Park on Sundays where they try to out-db each other to the great delight of hordes of school kids.

〔医者〕

　社会的地位があまりに高いせいか、平民の質問にはぜったい答えない――たとえそれが「今、何時ですか？」であっても。患者のバッグに入りきらないほどたくさんのクスリを処方して、こう言うのだ。「X剤は病気を治して、Y薬はX剤の副作用防止。Y薬の副作用はZ錠でおさえます。さらにA薬を飲めば、だいぶ気分がよくなりますよ」。豪華な巣に住んでいる。

《醫生大人》

　　也許是社會地位過高，他們絕對不會回答平民們所問的不相干問題，例如：「現在幾點？」。開出的藥方多到幾乎裝不進患者的皮包，他們的理由是：「X劑能治病，Y藥可防止X劑的副作用，Y藥的副作用靠Z錠抑制。另外，如果再加上吃A藥的話，會變得比較舒服。」這種族類都住在豪華別墅中。

The Doctor

High on the pecking order of society, this breed does not answer questions—even, "What time is it?" Will dispense more pills, potions and powder than you can carry in one bag with the words, "X will fix the ailment, Y will fix side effects of X, Z will fix side effects of Y and A is just to make you feel good." Live in well padded nests.

〔月曜の朝のゾンビ〕

　乗車率３００％の超満員電車に乗っているおかげで、よろける心配もつり革につかまる必要もない人々。デオドラント・スプレーのさわやかな香りがする人ゼロ。１，０００人中；無臭２００人、タバコ臭いの８００人、シャンプーの匂い５００人、ニンニクか昨夜の酒臭いの２０人、香水０．０００１人（重複回答あり）。

《週一早上的殭屍族》

　　乘坐在載客率達300％的爆滿電車，這些人可以慶幸不用擔心摔倒也不須抓著吊環。沒有一個人帶有除臭噴劑的清爽香味。每1,000人中，沒有臭味的約爲200人、菸臭味的有800人、聞起來帶有洗髮精香味的有500人、大蒜味或前晚酒臭的有20人，有香水味的只有那麼0.00001人（複選作答）。

Monday Morning Zombies

Travel in containers like train carriages and busses, packed to 300 percent of normal capacity to prevent them falling over and so they don't have to strap-hang. Totally ignore others around them, even if pressed tightly against them. None have B.O. Smells per 1,000: nothing 200, tobacco 800, soap and/or shampoo 500, garlic or stale booze 20, perfume 0.00001.

〔人間国宝〕

国民にとっても尊敬されている高齢の人たちで、みんなキモノを着ている。クシャクシャ髪かハゲ頭、そして一様に愛煙家。彼らは昔の言葉を使うので、テレビのインタビューでは字幕が必要となる。毎年新しく人間国宝になる人数よりも多く他界してしまうため、少数生物である。

《長壽國寶》

　　廣受民眾尊敬的高齡族群，都穿著和服，不是蓬鬆著頭髮，就是無髮，並都是愛菸家。由於他們都常使用古典的語彙，因此有時電視訪問時都必須打出字幕。因爲每年成爲新國寶的長壽級人數都比到另一個世界的少，故屬於較稀有生物。

The Living Treasure

A very highly respected member of the species who are quite old and always wear kimono which appear to be of similar age. Unkempt or bald, they all smoke, rarely smile and often talk in very ancient tongues so that on TV interviews it is necessary to have subtitles. They are endangered because they appear to die out faster than they are created.

〔携帯電話男〕

　急増中のこの人種、人混みの真っ只中に立ちはだかり、えんえんとしゃべり続けるツワモノである。屋内においては、たとえ高級クラブにいても窓際に立ち通しで、発信音にパブロフの犬のごとく反応する。スノッブなレストランでは、大変ひんしゅくをかっている人々。

《大哥大族》

　這種族人數正急速增加，常在擁擠的人潮中，滔滔不絕的講著電話，不介意妨礙到他人的前進。此外進入室內後，就算是高級俱樂部也會一直站在窗邊，對電話鈴聲也如同條件反射的狗兒一般異常敏感。在高級餐廳中，常惹人討厭。

The Pocket Phone Jack

This breed is on the increase and can be often found standing totally still in the middle of the sidewalk, chattering incessantly. Other times they are usually caught standing by windows, even in expensive nightclubs and respond to bleeps like Pavlov's dog. They have been recently banned from using their skills in most posh restaurants.

〔教育ママ〕

生存競争本能の権化。彼女たちの子供は、勉強漬けで窒息寸前である。ふつうの学校教育では満足できず、早朝に塾、放課後に塾、そして夜も塾へと子供を追い立てる。かくして、深夜や週末の電車で立ったまま居眠りする、制服姿のあわれな子供たちができ上がる。子供が大学入試に落ちた時、ママはいったいどうなるのだろう。

《教育媽媽》

生存競爭之下本能產生的質變。她們的孩子被填鴨般的學習，逼得快喘不過氣。此外又對一般學校教育不具信心，趕著孩子早上補習、放學後也補，晚上再補。結果造就一群穿著制服、在深夜和週末電車上站著打瞌睡的可憐孩童。眞不知這些孩子大學聯考落榜時，這些媽媽們會是什麼模樣。

The Education Mama

Filled with competitive instinct, this breed tends to smother their chicks with learning. Unsatisfied with a simple school curriculum, will force their chicks to attend pre-school school, after-school school and night school. Offspring can often be found asleep standing up on late night and weekend transport, dressed in their school uniform. It is not clear what happens to the Mama if her chick fails to gain university entrance.

〔社内のお荷物〕

どの会社にも必ず1人はいる。社長の級友だったという手合いが多く、タバコをふかして何杯もお茶をすする以外の仕事はあまりしていない。年功序列制度によって生き残り続けている。その制度によれば、ある年齢に達して困難になってきた職務から、全くできないので誰からも期待されない職務へと、昇進するようである。

《公司的負擔－窗邊族》

任何公司必定有一位，多爲總經理同學或是好友之類的人，除了抽菸和不停泡茶之外，不怎麼做事。靠著依年資升等的制度，依然可在公司生存。根據這個制度，只要達到一定年齡，便可以離開已無法勝任的職務，並可調升。因爲完全外行，因此不會被做太多的要求。

The Permanent Office Fixture

There is one of these in every office. Most often an old school chum of the president, they appear to do little else than smoke and demand repeated refilling of their tea cups. This breed is spawned by the corporate seniority system which states, once a person reaches a suitable age, they are automatically promoted out of a job they can't do well into a job which they can't do at all.

〔アンパイヤ〕

　野球試合をするための必要悪。視野に問題があり、カントクという敵に攻撃されると手をバタバタさせるので、祖先はコウモリ男だったとの説がある。語彙は乏しく、「ストラーイク！」か、もっと頻繁に発する「アーウト！」の呪いの言葉のみである。テレビでインタビューされることはまれで、球団の冬のキャンプに招かれることはさらにまれである。

《裁判》

　棒球比賽時必要的惡人。視力常有問題，當被教練般的敵人攻擊時，手會不停的拍動並揮舞，也有人說他們的祖先是蝙蝠。使用的語彙相當貧乏，例如「（好球）"STORE-RA-EEKU"」，或是更頻繁的使用的是如詛咒般的用語「（出局）"AW-TO!"」。很少被電視台訪問，更不會被邀請參加球隊冬季集訓活動。

The Umpire

A necessary evil which was spawned with the baseball cult/ritual. Some believe they are from the bat family due to their poor eyesight and also because they tend to get into a flap when confronted. Only have a limited vocabulary, punctuated by the two oaths, "Store-ra-ee-ku" and more often, "Aw-to"! Are very rarely interviewed on TV and never invited to summer or winter camps.

〔マッサージ師〕

しかるべき地域で活躍する、似た名前の職業の女性と混同しないように。こちらの方は温泉やサウナ周辺がテリトリー。強靭な指で、肉をはがさずに軟骨を骨からはずす神ワザをこなし、客の悲痛なわめき声を無上の悦びとする。彼らにもんでもらったあと３日間は、自宅で安静にしているほうが利口というものだ。

《按摩大師》

　　爲避免和類似名稱的馬殺雞女郎混淆，只活躍於適當的地區。這個族群的地盤是在溫泉和三溫暖附近，手指強勁有力，擅長不需剝開肌肉，便能將軟骨自骨骼中鬆開的神奇絕技，客人痛苦的慘叫聲是他們最大的喜悅。被他們按摩過後三天之內，最好在家中靜養爲宜。

The Masseur

Not to be confused with the female types operating in certain select areas of Japan, this male version can be found close by hot springs and bath houses. Equipped with tenacious talons, they are capable of detaching gristle from bone without tearing the flesh and appear to revel in the howls of agony from their clients. Don't plan to do anything for three days after a session.

〔百歳以上の高齢者〕

この最高齢集団は、なんと年々増え続けている。大阪より東京に多く、片田舎には意外と少ない。ということは、公害がひどいほど老人の健康にはよいようである。公害排斥運動家や嫌煙家にとって、少々都合が悪いかもしれない事実だが………。

《百歳人瑞》

這個最高齡集團的人數有逐年增加的趨勢。東京地區比大阪多，鄉下地方意外的反而較少。可能是公害愈嚴重，愈有益於老人的健康。對環保運動和拒吸二手菸的人士而言，這個族群也許和他們的論調恰好成了反證，有點矛盾。

The Centenarian

The real old crows of the species and their numbers are increasing annually. Per capita, there are more in Tokyo than in Osaka, and very few in the countryside. This has led to the firm belief that a high level of pollution contributes to living to a very old age, which is a bit of a serious setback for all the clean-air fanatics—as well as those strange folk who advocate non-smoking!

〔フツーの警官〕

武器は持っているものの、危険な存在ではない――自転車で通行人をひいたりしない限り。ガイジンは透明人間でもあるかのごとく無視する。拠点は交差点のちいさな小屋。信号の故障や交通事故があるたび、絶望的な渋滞をつくってあげるのが特技。この種の女性は、世界一小さな車に二人組で乗り、駐車違反を取締まっている。

《一般警官》

攜有武器，但除非騎腳踏車撞到行人，不具任何危險性。常把外國人當作透明人，完全忽視他們的存在。多據守在十字路口的小派出所。當交通號誌故障或發生交通事故時，製造嚴重交通阻塞是拿手好戲。如果是女性的話，大部份兩人一組，搭乘著世界最小的汽車，負責取締違法停車的人。

The Ordinary Policeman

Armed but rarely dangerous except if they ride into you on their bicycles. Appear to find foreigners transparent and breed in little hutches on most street corners. Very effective at creating chaotic traffic jams if traffic lights fail or if there is an accident. The female of the species can often be found in pairs in the tiniest of motor cars, hunting illegally parked vehicles.

〔機動隊の警官〕

顔のないこの人種、成田付近に生息しているようだが、外国の要人が来日するたびに都心にも現れる。移動する時は、窓に鉄の網を張った装甲車に乗り込む。話しかけられても決して口をきかず、ウワサによれば、きわめて暴力的でもあるという。

《鎮暴警察》

這種沒有臉部的族群似乎多生活在成田機場附近，遇到外國大人物到日本時，也會在東京都內出現。移動時多搭乘窗上設有鐵網的鎮暴車。就算和他們搭訕，也絕不會回話，據說都極具暴力傾向。

The Riot Policeman

Faceless, this species seems to breed at Narita Airport, however can often be found in cities whenever overseas VIP's are visiting. They are moved about in battleship grey busses with windows wired up to retain them. Never speak even if spoken to and by reputation, exceedingly violent.

〔ミス・ナントカ〕

　この国の女性の中では、最も見ためがよく、大変曲線的な体の持ち主たちである。いまだ男性優位なのか、この女性たちを生み出すコンテストはゴマンとある——ミス・〇〇〇リゾートという高尚なものから、ミス・×××トイレ用品メーカーなんて馬鹿げたのまで。いうまでもなく、彼女たちに求められる唯一の才能は、ハイレグ水着が似合うこと。

《某某選美小姐》

　　是日本女性中最好看且曲線玲瓏的族群。由於仍是男人主宰的社會，因此許多比賽的名稱都很荒謬，從高尚的某某休閒地小姐到可笑的某某衛浴用品小姐。顯然，她們所需具備的唯一條件是適合穿著高叉的泳裝。

Miss "Whatever"

The most gorgeous of the female members of the species and quite often, remarkable curvy. Due to the male dominance of the species, there are numerous contests to find these females and their titles range from the sublime to the ridiculous, from resort names to the names of sanitary equipment manufacturers! Apparently their only required talent is to be able to look good in "hi-cut" swimwear.

〔占い師〕

女性たちをいいカモにしているこの生物は、閉まった店や銀行の前にエラソーに陣取っている——夜でもサングラスをかけて。手相や棒きれやカードで彼らに占ってもらうウン勢は料金もウンと高い。インチキな英語の看板を揚げているのには要注意。

《算命仙》

　　這種生物最會欺騙女性，常在已打烊的商店和銀行前設攤，滿臉高傲之氣獨自坐在小桌後面，縱使是夜晚，也戴著墨鏡。透過他們看手相、抽籤和紙牌測得的命運都很好，但所需費用也水漲船高。有寫著蹩腳英文招牌的，多爲黑店，可要小心。

The Fortune Teller

Preyed upon by the females of the species, these creatures sit in solitary splendor at small tables in disused shop and bank doorways, wearing dark glasses —even at night. They read palms, sticks and cards plus charge a fortune to read a fortune. The most famous one in Tokyo bears a sign stating, "Ingrish Spoking"!

〔庭師〕

　B級ホラー映画の登場人物のようで、コワイ人たち、ボンサイストより危険性のある彼らは、剪定の練習ももっぱら自宅で行う。切った枝は、ていねいに「普通ゴミ」サイズに束ねるところが裏ワザ。日本にはほとんど土がないため、すきはあまり使わない。

《園藝師》

　　像限制級恐怖片出現的可怕人物。比盆栽師更具危險性，專在自己家中練習剪枝。會細心地把剪下的樹枝捆綁成普通垃圾的大小。由於日本幾乎沒有土，很少使用鋤頭。

The Gardener

A frightening breed, they look like characters from a second-rate horror movie. More tenacious than the Bonsai-ist they often only have minute little lairs in which to practice their pruning. Scrupulously tidy, they will pick up every tiny thing they clip and neatly tie it into bundles of precise size for disposal. Rarely operate spades because there is not enough earth.

〔くみ取り車の作業員〕

独特な臭いですぐわかるこの人種は、テクノロジーの発達とともに都会から姿を消しつつある。とはいえ、家が田んぼに囲まれている地域では、いまだ健在――「結局、誰かがやらなきゃいけないんだ……」とブツブツ言いながらも。極東の他の国々の同業者に比べ、今後の生活は保証されていない。

《水肥收集車作業員》

只要聞到特殊異味，便知道是這個人種，隨著科技的發達，已逐漸從都市中消失。但仍存在於房舍四周都是田野的區域，他們常常抱怨著說，這種工作終究還是要有人做。和其他遠東國家的同行比，未來的生活較沒有保障。

The Honeywagon Engineer

Detectable by day or night due to their distinctive odor, these are a breed which is rapidly disappearing from cities as technology about pumping the product uphill is advancing. Still to be seen/smelt in areas where homes are constructed among rice fields. If approached, will grunt, "Well somebody's gotter do it!" Not as financially secure as their counterparts in the Far East.

〔ゴルフ狂〕

　公営ゴルフ場で1ラウンドたった1万5千円（たったのだって！？）でプレーするためならば、午前2時からの行列もいとわない。週末には必ず、さもいとおしそうにクラブを磨く。これまでにプレーしたどのゲームのどのショットをも、克明に覚えている人々。コースを予約できなかった日でも、喜々として打ちっぱなしを楽しんでいる。

《高爾夫球狂》

　　爲了到公營球場打一回「只要」1萬5千日圓的高爾夫球，不在乎從半夜兩點開始排隊。每逢週末必然會清理球桿和擦亮球體。這種人會清楚的記著到目前爲止，在某場球局中，擊出過什麼樣的球。縱然在預約不到球場的日子，也會興高采烈的討論著打球的趣聞。

The Golf-aholic

Will willingly join a queue at 2 a.m., to play one round on a public golf course, which costs only ¥15,000 (Only!). Spends every weekend, lovingly cleaning his clubs and putting a shine on his balls. Can recite every stroke at every game he has played and if unable to get a game, will merrily hit balls into the air at a practice range, day or night.

〔ウサギ小屋〕

居住者のプライバシーなどないに等しいことから、鳥カゴとも呼ばれている。この国の人々が、背が低く、正座ができ、毎朝フトンをたたみ、盆栽を生み出したのは、この小さな住空間のせいであるという者も多い。しかしこんなの、ニワトリか卵かと同じ問題じゃないか！

《兔窩小屋》

由於居住者幾乎毫無隱私權，又被稱爲鳥籠。許多人認爲，狹小的居住空間是造成這個國家的人長得不高、能夠跪坐、每天折收棉被及能做出盆栽的原因。不過這種論調不是又會扯出類似先有雞，還是先有蛋的問題嗎？

The Rabbit Hutch

These dwellings are often called "bird cages" due to the walls giving just about the same level of privacy to the occupants. This tiny area in which to live has created the myth about this being the reason why the species are rather short in stature, can sit with their legs folded up, roll up their beds in the day and cultivate bonsai. It's a matter of which came first!

〔仲人オバサン〕

何世紀にもわたり、未婚の子供を持つ親の強力な味方となってきた。昔は男女の縁をとりもつ唯一の存在として活躍したが、現在では他にも手段があるので、影が薄くなりつつある。コンピューター結婚相談所は豊富なデータで成果をあげているし、なんとホントに恋愛する人も多くなったとか。

《媒人婆婆》

　　幾世紀以來，對家有未婚子女的父母來說，是重要的存在。以前的婚姻僅能靠她們來牽線，可以說是相當風光，不過現在有其他的方法，因此相對的也就日漸式微了。事實上目前電腦婚姻介紹所有極豐富的資料，效果也不錯，大有人因此而墜入愛河，而撮合配對成功的例子也還眞不少呢。

The Matchmaker

This particular group has been around for centuries, proffering assistance to the parents of unwed offspring. Once they were the only method used to match pairs, however nowadays, various other means are used as well. Computerization has appeared allowing huge data banks to be created of those wishing to meet each other; also, many of the species now actually fall in love.

〔銭湯〕
　まるで鳥のようだが、日本には公衆浴場が存在する。現代ではまれになったが、昔は混浴が多かったそうで、うらやましい限り。近所のウワサ話を楽しみ、上司や奥方をしばし忘れてくつろぐために、煮え湯のような熱さをものともせず、人々はここに集うのである。

《錢湯（公共浴室）》
　很不可思議的在日本有公共澡堂的存在，到了現代當然是少了許多，據說以前還有很多男女共浴的澡堂，實在令人羨慕。在「錢湯」一邊洗澡一邊談論他人長短，輕輕鬆鬆地暫時把上司或太座拋諸腦後，也是種享受。雖然浴池內的水像煮沸的水一般燙，但是人們還是帶著自己的浴具（洗髮精等），來此報到。

Sentō

The public bird bath of the species. Once for mixed sexes, those types are rare nowadays. Irrespective of the heat of the water, the species will gather daily in a ritualistic manner to launder the local gossip and to relax after a hard day avoiding the boss, wife, etc. Regulars always carry their own shampoo.

〔男子中・高生〕

ふくらんだカバンを肩に掛け、小さな集団で通学する。ファーストフードの到来以降、彼らの身長はみるみる伸びた。制服は古臭い軍服のようだが、クツの方はかかとを踏みつぶしてスリッパのようなのが興味深い。

《高中男生》

　　肩上掛著鼓鼓的書包，以小集團的方式通學。自從速食餐飲引進之後，他們的身高也有可觀的成長。制服像是呆板的軍服，而鞋子卻故意踩著腳後跟部分，弄得像是穿拖鞋似的，這點倒頗有趣。

The Schoolboy Commuter

Carries a bulging shoulder bag and travels in small groups. Since the advent of fast foods, this species has become startlingly tall. They retain the plumage of ancient Japanese militia, however their footwear usually has the heel kicked down and is worn like a slipper.

〔ハゲ頭の抵抗〕

他の日本人は彼と同じくらいの背丈なのでよく見えないが、やや背の高いガイジンはこの人種を見やぶってしまう。「ススキ頭」という幻視トリックを使っているが、上から見下ろせば、これはバーコード以外の何物でもない。まわりの人たちより、いち早く雨が降り始めたことがわかる。頭皮に降る雨は、意外とウルサイのである。

《光頭族》

由於其他的日本人同這類族群一般高，可能看不清楚，若是由較高的外國人來觀察則一下就看到了真相。或許有些人會使用假髮來障眼，但由上往下看時，除了如條碼般稀疏幾根之外，什麼也沒有。這類族群比一般人更早知道什麼時候開始下雨。雨點打在頭上時，能比別人快察覺，且對下在頭上的雨，非常在意。

BALD IS
BEAUTIFUL

The Bald Ego

Because most natives are relatively the same height, this species is most often noticed by foreigners who are slightly taller. Strands of hair are laid across the bald pate to create the illusion of thatch. Their appearance from above is identical to the Universal Product Code label number, 6-123456789 0-2. They can hear rain before most others notice it is raining.

〔オバサン〕

どんなに混んだバスや電車でも、難なく乗り降りできる人々のこと。もしあなたが満員電車で身動きがとれなくなったら、オバサンについて行けばよい。カサや買物袋やひじテツで簡単に通り道を作っていくのだから。また、彼女たちの毒舌はすさまじいので注意されたし。いずれにせよ、「オバサン恐るべし」！

《歐巴桑》

這族群在無論是多麼擁擠的巴士或在電車上下車時，都如履平地。當您在滿載乘客的電車裏動彈不得時，只要緊跟在歐巴桑後頭下車，必定倍覺輕鬆愉快。她們會用傘、購物袋或手肘的功夫簡簡單單地殺出一條通道來。此外，她們的舌頭帶有毒性，非常厲害，不可不小心提防。總而言之，千萬不要去招惹她們。

The Oba-san

Can enter and exit any level of crowded conveyance. Deft with umbrellas, shopping bags or just plain elbows, if you are stuck in a rush hour train just follow the swathe they carve through the mob. They are equipped with a sharp tongue and can castigate any species with equal venom. Add a new dimension to the term, "Sweet little old ladies"!

〔オリンピックをめざす少年少女〕

　また幼いヒヨコたちだが、生まれた時から競争精神をたたきこまれている。「金を勝ち取れ」という言葉が、まだ話せないうちから耳の中で鳴り響いている。公園や公営プールで、熱心すぎる親に激励されながら練習に明け暮れる日々。だがそのほとんどは長じて平凡な会社員となり、選手になるものはごく少数である。

《奥林匹克小先鋒》

　雖然年紀尚小，但打從乳臭未乾時即被灌輸競賽精神。在還不會開口說話之際，「立志拿金牌」這句話早已如雷灌耳深植腦中，在狂熱父母親的激勵之下，每天不斷在公園或市營的游泳池從早到晚拼命練習。不過這樣成長的孩子，長大後幾乎都成了平凡的公司職員，能當上選手的少之又少。

The Olympian

Startlingly young, these chicks are imbued with the competitive spirit from birth. "Go for the Gold" rings in their ears almost before they are able to talk. Can be seen at every park and public swimming pool, usually pursued by at least one parent, shouting encouragement. Most grow into salarymen or OL's and a few into athletes.

〔ちびっ子タレント〕

例外なく歯並びが悪いのに、始終ニッコリと笑顔をつくる少女たちのこと。驚くほど冷静で自己をコントロールできるため、何でもやってのける。単に歩いてみせたり、自分の手でつかめないくらい大きなマイクで「歌」と称するものを披露したり・・・・。驚くべきことに、彼女たちの多くは、実はかなりのレベルの才能をもっている。

《幼齒明星》

毫無例外每個人牙齒的排列極不整齊，但隨時保持著微笑。令人訝異的是非常冷靜，且能自我控制得很好，因此做什麼都有板有眼。走台步、握著比自己手掌還大的麥克風載歌載舞等........。更教人吃驚的是，在她們之中有很多確實是具有相當才華的。

The Child Actress

All appear to have mis-cast teeth and smile continuously. This species is amazingly calm and self-controlled when doing anything from simply walking around to "singing" into a microphone bigger than they can grasp in one hand. Surprisingly, quite a number of them have a remarkable level of talent.

〔ビア・ジョッキ〕

　この容器にはいろいろなサイズとデザインが出回っているが、どれも入る量に差などなさそうである。泡の表面がふちまで来ていて、把手の上まで液体が入ってさえいれば、満杯だとされてしまう。ビールが人間関係の潤滑油となっているこの国では、毎年、４大メーカーがそれぞれ少なくとも５種類は新製品を発売する。それにしても「禁酒の」ビールとは、きついシャレのつもりか！？

《啤酒杯》

　　這種容器有許許多多的尺寸及樣式，不過容量方面大同小異。將酒倒到把手上方，使泡沫漲滿杯緣，這樣叫做滿杯。在日本，啤酒無異是人際關係的最佳潤滑油，每年四大廠商至少要推出五種新產品問世。儘管如此，「禁酒」（Dry　Beer）這個名詞，竟然一語雙關，還是最暢銷的名牌哩。

Beer Jokki

A container available in many different sizes which all appear to hold the same amount of liquid. They are considered full when the froth reaches the rim and the beer, the top of the handle. As beer is one of the major lubricants of the species, the four brewers constantly compete by introducing new brands—often 5 each every year. Surely, "dry beer" is a contradiction of words?!

〔魚の競売〕

夜明け前に築地魚市場へ行って何百人の競り手に混じってみよう。しかし調子に乗りすぎてうっかり手を上げたりすると、自分の身長より長い魚を買い取るハメになる。どうにか地下鉄に乗れたとしても、自宅の冷蔵庫に収まるわけがないではないか。

《魚市競賣》

建議您不妨於破曉時分走一趟魚市場,體驗一下混入幾百個競相喊價、標購的魚販群中的感覺,只是千萬不要過於投入而不自覺的舉起手跟人喊價,搞得可能會買到一條比自己身高還要長的大魚的結局,即使有辦法拎著魚擠地下鐵回家,但家裏的冰箱可不一定放得下去喔。

The Fish Buyer

Before dawn's early light, take a trip to Tsukiji fish market and join the hundreds of bidders. Don't raise your hand or you might become the proud owner of a fish, longer than you are tall. Embarrassing on the subway and as difficult as heck to stuff into your refrigerator.

〔英会話学校の生徒〕

片時もテキストを離さず、ガイジンにまとわりついては話しかけてくる。それも、会話レッスン用テープそっくりの話し方で。大半はアメリカ英語だが、昨今はオーストラリアやフランス、ドイツのなまりがあったり、驚くべきことにクイーンズ・イングリッシュを話す者までいる。

《英語中心裏的學生》

　　片刻也不離課本，死纏著「老外」來作會話練習。而且所講的語句與會話教學用的錄音帶還眞是沒兩樣。講的大半是美式英語，最近學生們的發音居然還有澳洲腔、法國腔或德國腔，更教人吃驚的是居然有人會講一口字正腔圓的正統英語。

The English Student

Tend to follow foreigners and rarely seen without a textbook in hand. Will speak without being spoken to and sound remarkably like pre-recorded tapes. Most have American accents, but these days, a few with Australian, French, German and even English accents can be heard.

〔夜の図書館〕

駅周辺には必ずある。独身男性にとって、自分の選んだ本を他人に知られることなく、夜の読書タイムを充実させてくれる強い味方だ。英語版は一冊もないが、どうせ文章なんて読む必要はないので、きちんと役に立つ。こういう「雑誌」は地味な紙で包まない限り、人前で持ち歩かないように。

《深夜圖書館》

　　　車站附近一定可以找得到。當一個單身男性不想讓別人知道自己在看什麼樣的書籍，而又想養眼時，這裡是最佳選擇。雖然沒有英文版的，但對外國人來說反正也不需要讀文章所以沒差。但是這類「雜誌」若沒有用紙包起來，最好不要攜帶它在他人面前走動。

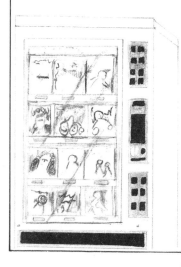

Late Night Library

Found by nearly every railway station, this is a chance for the lone wolf to pick his night time reading without others seeing what he chooses. None of the publications are in English; mind you most of them don't need any descriptive text at all. These "magazines" are never carried in public without them being in plain, brown paper covers.

〔おにぎり〕

「ライス・ボール」といったって、子供が握ったのでもない限り、球形はしていない。日本人の主食の一つであり、のりで包んだのが一般的。中身のほうは多様でガイジンにも食べられるもの（ツナ）もあれば、いろいろな国の食べ物を経験してきたツワモノでも敬遠するもの（納豆）もある。

《飯糰》

　　雖然英文翻譯成「Rice Ball」，但只要不是由小孩來捏，是不會成球狀的。爲日本人的主食之一，通常外表會裹一片海苔。裏面包的餡就各式各樣了，有外國人愛吃的鮪魚飯糰，也有連吃遍各國食品百毒不侵的「勇伯」都敬謝不敏的「納豆」飯糰，你要不要也嚐一個？

The Rice Ball

Never in the shape of a ball, unless made by children, these are almost the staple diet of the nation. Wrapped in a sheet of dried kelp, the contents vary from items most foreigners would consider edible (cooked tuna) to some things, even a hardened traveller would prefer not to put in their mouth (*nattō*).

〔大学生〕

　この人種はみな、タバコを吸いパチンコと麻雀をやり、そして何より絶対に勉強などしない。大学周辺や駅、アイスクリーム屋とかファーストフード店にたむろしている。お金はあるようだが、外ではあまり酒を飲まないようだ。

《大學生》

　　這類族群不是叼著煙、就是沈醉於打柏青哥或麻將，最重要的是絕對不讀書。他們不是聚集在學校附近或車站的冷飲店中，就是在速食店裡磨牙。看起來頗富有，但通常不會在外面喝酒。

The College Student

This breed appears to smoke, play pachinko and mahjong and never ever study. Can be found in crowds, milling about in front of universities, nearby railway stations, ice cream parlors and fast food outlets. Most appear to have money, but surprisingly few drink alcohol in public.

〔大学入試〕

大学に入るために必ず受けなければならない、拷問のようなもの。予備校を繁盛させ夜間働く講師たちを養うために毎年2月に政府が主催するイベントである。

《大學聯招》

　　就如同嚴刑拷打的試煉一般，要進大學就非得通過這關不可。這是日本政府為了振興補習教育、增加夜間教師就業機會，而於每年2月所主辦的大型活動。

Exam Hell Ritual

The annual Right of Passage ritual which is pressure-induced torture to gain a position at any university. Held every February, it appears to be a Government sponsored tradition to keep cram schools in business and feather the nests of unemployed teachers who work at night.

〔高校野球〕

テレビカメラと全国の視聴者を喜ばせるために行う、年2回の催し。広告スペースを提供し、暇な野球解説者に仕事を与える以外には、有益な目的はないようだ。

〈高中棒球〉

爲了滿足觀眾出現在全國的電視攝影機前，每年舉行兩次的例行比賽。除了提供廣告的空間及讓那些游手好閒的棒球解說員餬口之外，似乎沒有其它實質意義。

High School Baseball Tourney Ritual

Twice every year, every high school is forced to play against each other for the pleasure of the television cameras and millions of viewers. Doesn't appear to serve any useful purpose, other than being a vehicle for advertising and giving out of work baseball commentators, something to do.

〔ニュースキャスター〕

　８０キロの交通渋滞から上野動物園のパンダまで、何についても異常にコーフンして語る人々。現場に残るチョークの線を指さして、事故について１０分間もしゃべり続けられるのはお見事。決して息が切れたりせず、普通の人より１オクターブ声も高い。

《新聞現場播報員》

　　從堵塞 80 公里的長龍到上野動物園的熊貓，不管播報什麼都可以說得口沫橫飛，興奮異常。指著現場用粉筆所留下的白線，針對小小的事件，就可滔滔不絕講上 10 分鐘；著實令人佩服，絕不會吃螺絲或中斷，且比起一般人的聲音還要高八度。

The TV Caster

Always exceedingly excited about everything from an 80 kilometer traffic jam to the latest antics of Ueno Zoo's pandas. Can spend 10 minutes talking about a traffic accident while pointing at chalk marks on the street. Never ever seem to get out of breath and keep their voices pitched an octave above the rest of the species.

〔ゴルフ・ウィドウ〕

皮肉なんかじゃなく、日本で一番幸せな女たち。夫は毎週末になると、早朝からゴルフに出かけて夜遅くまで帰ってこない。おかげで彼女たちは、ジャマをされずにやりたいことができるわけだ——洗たくとかフトン干しとか、そうじに料理などを。

《小白球寡婦》

　　絕不是挖苦，她們是全日本最幸福的女性。每到週末，先生一大早就去打高爾夫球直到深夜才會回來，也因爲如此，這些夫人們不會受打擾，可以做自己想做的事，譬如洗衣服、曬棉被或打掃煮飯等。

Golf Widow

Truly, the happiest of the female of the species. Her rooster disappears each Saturday and Sunday from before dawn to after dusk and usually returns to the nest tired but sober. She has the place to herself all weekend to do whatever she wants to—which is usually the laundry, or futon beating, or cleaning or cooking.

〔マンガ本〕

日本人はみなマンガ中毒である。このセリフ入り絵本の内容は多彩で、ＳＦや「会社のおこし方」などというのもあるが、多くは暴力とセックス過剰。子供向けのマンガとなると、星の数ほどもある。まだ小さな子供がマンガ本を面白そうに読む姿は、読めないガイジンにとって実にクヤシイのだ。

《漫畫》

日本人全國都中了漫畫毒。這種有故事情節的畫冊，內容精采萬分，從科幻到「創業經營指南」五花八門，但有許多是過分強調暴力及色情。至於小朋友的漫畫則有如天上繁星那麼多。看到小小年紀的孩童一副讀得入神的樣子，眞敎想看卻不懂日文的外國人爲之歎息。

The Comic Book

The addiction of the whole species, these picture books with words are about everything imaginable from pure science fiction to starting your own company and many are startlingly violent and/or pornographic. Children's versions abound and it is very irritating for foreigners to observe tiny kids who can actually read them!

〔買(か)い物(もの)客(きゃく)〕

収納(しゅうのう)スペースが十分(じゅうぶん)にないので、日本人(にほんじん)は毎日(まいにち)買(か)い物(もの)をする。外国(がいこく)と違(ちが)って、商品(しょうひん)はバラ売(う)りや小(しょう)パックで売(う)られ、また三重(さんじゅう)以上(いじょう)の過剰(かじょう)包装(ほうそう)が常識(じょうしき)。ただ一(ひと)つ極(きょく)小(しょう)サイズでないのは、16ロールもあるトイレットペーパー！本来(ほんらい)の使用(しよう)目的(もくてき)以外(いがい)、いったい何(なに)に使(つか)うというのだ。

《採購狂》

由於沒地方放置物品,日本人幾乎是每天購物。與外國不同的是,日本商品大多以散裝或小包裝在販售,而三層以上的過剩包裝在日本是一種常態。只有一種不是小包裝的,就是16捆裝的大包衛生紙,除了原來的使用目的之外,不知道還有什麼樣的用途?

The Shopper

Due to the incredible lack of storage space in the average nest, the species is a daily shopper. Goods are sold either singly or in Lilliputian sizes and often more than triple wrapped. A departure from the norm are toilet rolls which seem to come in packs of at least 16! It is unknown what other uses the species has for them.

〔銀行のロビー係〕

ひっきりなしに客にあいさつをするこの人種は、日本人が何か困っている様子だとすっ飛んで来るが、ガイジンが同じ状況にいる時は姿を消している。たとえ捕まえたとしても、英語は全く話さず、しきりに首を振ったり歯の間からシーシーと音をたてるのみ。自動振込機の操作を英語で説明できる者は皆無のようだ。

《銀行大廳人員》

　　這種不斷向客人問好並打躬作揖的人，一看到本國人有什麼困擾時就會飛奔過去幫忙解決，但當外國人遇到同樣的狀況時卻又不見他們的蹤影，即使逮到他們，他們也不會講英文，只會死命地搖頭、從牙齒間發出嘶、嘶的聲音。至於用英文說明怎麼使用自動提款機，更是沒有一個人會。

The Bank Lobby Lady

Always welcoming and bidding adieu to customers, this species is quick to appear beside any native having problems but usually vanishes if a foreigner gets into difficulty. Once captured, they can never speak English but shake their heads and suck their teeth a lot. Never seem to have machine instructions in English.

〔タテ型社会〕

日本は明確な序列社会だ。企業においては、ある年齢になると昇進の階段が用意されている。子供だって、学校や遊びの場で年の違う子たちと接することは少ない。言葉づかいすら、相手との上下関係によって変える。しかるに水平思考のできる者は、この社会を見限って脱出してしまう。

《垂直型社會》

日本是個明確的序列型的社會。在企業中，一旦到了某種年齡，昇進之路早就被安排好了，連孩童們在學校或遊樂場中也絕少與年齡不同的小孩接觸。即使是說話時，也會因對象的長幼關係而有所區別。因此能作水平思考的人們，往往會看破這個社會而出走。

Vertical Society

The pecking order in Japan is well defined: Progress in anything is straight up and down. When you are old enough, you automatically climb the corporate ladder. At school or at play, you never associate with those beyond your station in life, above or below. Even the language style used changes with the status of the talker and the talkee. Lateral thinkers appear to have flown the coup.

〔ソバをズルズルすする人〕

屋台やくつ箱ほどの大きさの店で、アツアツのソバをすすり上げるの姿は、昼夜問わず見かけられる。夜は酔っぱらいが酔いざましによく使う手段であるーー効果のほどはさまざまだが。自分の服をおシャカにする覚悟がない限り、あまり近寄って観察するのは避けた方がよろしい。

《吸麵族》

　　不管是白天或晚上，經常可在路邊小攤或像鞋櫃般大小的店裏看到一群人唏哩呼嚕地大口吸食著麵條。夜間的醉漢常用此來醒酒 － 雖然效果不一。除非你不害怕自己的衣服成了油星點點，否則建議你千萬別靠近。

The Noodle Slurper

Can be seen at any time of the day or night, noisily inhaling white hot noodles, either at streetside stalls or in shoebox-sized shops. In the evening, these are quite often nocturnal pub-crawlers trying not to become obnoxious drunks—with varying success. Should be observed from a distance unless you are planning to throw away your clothes.

〔経済学者〕

この人種はいつも、質問に質問で答える。5種類の通貨の為替レートを、コンマ3ケタまで正確に言えるのが自慢。将来についての確信は何もなく、市場を語るときは「オイル・ショック」だの「バブル経済」だのと便利な言葉を多用する。彼らが自分のおカネを少しでも投資しているのかどうかは、さだかではない。

《經濟學者》

　　這種人對問題的回答方式，就是再提出問題。他們以能正確地講出五種外幣的匯率直到小數點3位而引以為傲。對於未來趨勢則毫無把握，說明市場時，則常用「石油危機」或「泡沫經濟」等方便字眼。事實上他們是否是用自己口袋的錢在做投資，那就沒人知道了。

The Economist

This breed always answers questions with questions. Can quote exchange rates to three decimal places in five different currencies. They are never certain of the future and often mumble terms like, "Oil Shock" or "Bubble Economy" when talking about the money market. It is uncertain if they ever invest any of their own money.

〔結婚写真〕

子孫に残される、決まりきったポーズの写真。自分の子供がまた子供をつくって三世代ローンを組める確信がない限り、マイホームはぜったい無理だということを、写真の新婚夫婦の表情はもの語っている。最初の2年間は、挙式費用の返済に明け暮れる結婚生活でもある。

《結婚照》

此種傳家照片看起來都是擺同樣姿式。照片裏新婚夫婦的表情說明了一件事：若沒有孩子及孫子的三世共同貸款，不可能擁有自己的房子。甚至結婚兩年後，還得拼命工作償還婚禮費用的貸款哩。

The Wedding Photo

A stereotype pose, handed down from generation to generation, designed to show that the newlyweds are already aware they will never be able to own their own home unless they can have children who also have children, so that they can get a father, son and grandson mortgage. Spend the first two years of married life paying off the wedding ceremony debt.

〔海外旅行者〕

アンカレッジやシドニー、ＬＡ、スキポルなど世界中の免税店でお目にかかれる日本人のこと。年末年始とゴールデンウィーク、それとお盆休みに大挙して外国へ行く。海外に行かなかった友人のお土産に、大金を使って帰ってくる。

《海外旅行者》

指的是在安克拉治或雪梨、洛杉磯等各地的免税店中所看到的日本人。利用新年前後及黃金週或者暑假，大批前往國外，然後花大把鈔票並給那些未能出國的親友們帶些紀念品回來的人。

The Overseas Vacationer

The most well recognized member of the species which can be found in duty-free stores as far apart as Anchorage and Sydney, or Los Angles and

Schipol. Mostly migrate all together at New Year, Golden Week (May) and the summer *Obon* holiday (August) periods. Spend a lot of money, mostly on presents for those who don't go overseas.

〔自転車〕

　警告ブレーキなる秘密兵器でキーキーといやな音を立てるこの機械は、駅前にたくさん放置されている。警察が時たま排除するものの、数日後にはまた、同じ状態に戻ってしまう。歩道を走る自転車は、通行人の安全を大いに脅かしている。

《自行車》

　　　每當煞車時就會發出如秘密武器般令人討厭的警告聲響「嘰---！嘰---！」。這種機械，大量的被擱置在車站前面。雖然警察偶爾會拖吊，但沒幾天又會恢復原狀。跑在人行道上的腳踏車對於行人無異是一大威脅。

The Bicycle

Fitted with advanced-warning brake pads whose squeak can dislodge every tooth filling in your head, these machines congregate around stations, are cleared away by the police from time to time and reappear immediately. Ridden along the footpath, they have priority over pedestrians and are exceedingly dangerous.

〔陸上選手〕

　この人種の体は骨と皮と筋肉だけでできているので、まるで大飢饉のあった国から来た難民のように見える。日本では毎週のようにマラソン大会が行われるが、気の毒なことだ。先導する白バイの排気ガスを大量に吸って体重を減らしてしまう選手たちは、回復する余裕もないにちがいない。

《田徑選手》

　　由於這種人的體格僅由骨架及皮膚和筋肉構成，所以活像是從某個剛發生大饑荒國度裏逃出來的難民。在日本幾乎每週都有舉辦馬拉松。說來還真令人同情；像這樣常常吸著前導車所排放出來的大量廢氣因而體重不斷下降的選手們，又怎會有充分時間去恢復體重呢？

The Athlete

Constructed of skin, bone and muscles, this breed always looks like some refugee from a famine plagued land. In Japan there are marathons almost every week, so these athletes never get much time to regain the weight they lose by jogging behind police motorbikes, inhaling photochemical fog.

〔ヘビー・スモーカー〕

　この国（くに）では、喫煙（きつえん）はごく自然（しぜん）な行為（こうい）。一日（いちにち）4箱（はこ）に及（およ）ぶ者（もの）もいるが、そのほとんどは少（すこ）しふかしてはもみ消（け）しているようだ。近頃（ちかごろ）、ＪＲ山手線（やまてせん）のホームでは「喫煙所（きつえんじょ）」へと追（お）いやられている。何故（なぜ）なら、ただ灰皿（はいざら）をなくしただけでは、彼（かれ）らは少（すこ）しもひるまなかったからである―― 吸（す）いがらは線路（せんろ）に投（な）げ捨（す）てていたのだ。

《重型菸槍》

　　　在這個國度裏吸菸是最自然的行爲。有人甚至一天四盒，但通常一根菸沒吸幾口就丟掉。最近在ＪＲ山手線的月台上，吸菸者都會被趕到「吸菸處」。因爲就算沒有菸灰缸也難不倒他們，他們的菸蒂早已隨手丟在沿路的鐵軌上了。

The Heavy Smoker

A natural habit of the species, some can reach four packs a day, but often only take a couple of puffs and then put the cigarette out. Now, this breed has been officially relegated to "Smoking Zones" on the JR Yamanote Line when authorities found out that simply removing the ashtrays didn't stop them. They merely threw the butts on the tracks.

〔ファッション〕

長かったキモノ文化の反動で、自己表現する洋服が台頭した。とはいえ「渋カジ」と「オート・クチュール」は演歌とロックほどの差があるのも否めない。ときどき、ブランド名やロゴに呆れるほどまちがった英語を使っている。

《流行服飾》

　　　長時間在「和服文化」奴役下的反彈，致使能表現自我的西洋服飾抬頭。但不能否認的是，從澀谷「新人類的休閒服飾」到「高級時裝」之間就像是演歌與流行樂曲間有很大的差別。有時品牌名及商標上常可發現到非常多的錯誤英文。

The Fashion Statement

A backlash against the traditional kimono has caused a wave of this expressive clothing to appear. Termed the "Youth Culture Fashion" it has about as much resemblance to "Haute Couture" as *enka* songs have to rock and roll. Some astonishing use of English can be discovered by the serious observer.

〔同時通訳者〕

音声を出す機械のような人々。話す者の思考パターンを先読みして、聞くと同時に話すことができる。日本語は最後の一字でイキナリ質問文に変貌するため、英語に通訳しているほうは、あわてて" Isn't it ?"（ですね？）と付け加えることになるのだ。

《同步翻譯員》

像是會發出聲音的機械。他們先解讀說話者的思考模式，然後便可一邊聽一邊同步翻譯。由於日語表現上常會於句尾突然變成疑問句，所以在翻譯時會使用這招：趕快加上這句"Isn't it ?"（不是嗎？）

Simultaneous Translator

Sound operated voice machines, this breed can think ahead into the thought pattern of those they are listening to and talk at the same time as they are listening. Because a Japanese sentence can turn into a question with the very last syllable, the speakers sometimes end a statement with the words, "Isn't it?"

〔バイクに乗ったテロリスト〕

暴走族と呼ばれ、外見も手ごわそうである。マフラーを取り、エンジン全開で夜の静寂をぶちこわしてくれる。集団行動が大好きな彼らだが、日中はあまり活動しない。というのも渋滞がひどくて、自転車に乗ったおまわりさんにパクられてしまうからである。

《暴走族（機車恐怖份子）》

一般被稱做暴走族的人，外型也令人害怕，且不易驅散。夜晚，這些「暴走族」取下消音器，把引擎開到最高轉速，劃破安靜的深夜街頭。有時獨自一人，但更喜歡結隊做團體行動，白天他們不太會出現在交通擁擠的街道，因為會被騎腳踏車的警察甕中捉鱉。

Motorcycle Terrorist

A breed that appears almost impossible to stamp out, these *bōsōzoku* bozos drive around quiet streets at night, engines at full rev, with no mufflers. Sometimes alone but often in a group, they never appear to operate on the normal streets where the traffic jams would allow the policeman on his push-bike to catch them!

〔忘年会〕

毎年、師走になると催される酒盛り。三次会を過ぎた頃には、体がぐにゃぐにゃになりながらも、必死に重力に抵抗している人々が見かけられる。途中でカラオケ大会と化し、最終的には皆へべれけになって家路につくのがお決まりのコース。

《忘年會》

　　　每年 12 月的聯歡酒會。一個晚上喝到「換場」三次之後，可以瞧見一群人雖然已醉得雙腳發軟，但還勉強對抗地心引力似的搖擺在街頭。接著可能還要去卡拉 OK 鬧一陣子，往往喝得酩酊大醉後才會回家。

Bōnenkai

Traditional, year-end gift giving and party time. After the third party the same evening, some can be seen in small groups who can defy gravity although their bodies appear to lack any bones. Often change into some form of karaoke warbler for a period before finally emerging as Greater or Lesser Obnoxious Drunks for the trip home.

〔時代劇俳優〕

いつもオソロシイ形相をしていて、笑顔をふりまいたりはしない。チャンバラ・シーンでは、自分の背後を透視する能力を発揮する。わき役に比べて2オクターブも声が低く、反対に背は高くてスマート。殺される時は、長い長い時間をかけて息をひきとる。キス・シーンは演じない。

〈「鏘芭樂」時代劇的主角〉

　　從不露笑容而且看起來眞得令人十分懾服。比武時似乎具有透視身後任何風吹草動的超能力。他們的聲音比配角要低兩個八度，通常身材高挑而且極度健康。即使受重傷往往需要耗費多時才會斷氣。喔，還有他們從來不拍接吻的鏡頭。

Samurai Actor

Never smile and really look quite frightening. Appear to be able to see through the back of their heads when engaged in swordfights. Their voices are pitched two octaves below the other actors, and they are usually taller and incredibly fit. If killed, take a very long time to die. Never kiss.

〔ラグビー選手〕

　ワラビーズやオール・ブラックスに交じると、子供のように小さく見える。それでもホンコン・セブンスでは熱狂的な応援を受けている――たいてい負けてしまうが。週末、若い選手たちが河川敷で練習に打ち込んでいるのをよく見る。真冬には、泥まじりの雪にまみれてまで。

《橄欖球選手》

　　站在澳洲瓦拉比隊或是紐西蘭黑人隊旁顯得十分瘦小，這個族群在參加香港七人橄欖球賽時，雖受到瘋狂加油，但卻經常敗北。週末常可見年輕的選手在河邊練球，即使是遍地積雪的嚴冬也是如此。

The Rugby Player

Look very tiny when alongside Wallabies or All Blacks, this species is cheered wildly at the Hong Kong Sevens—but usually lose. Younger ones can be found at any weekend, practicing their art on riverbanks—even in mid winter with snow on the ground.

〔お見合い〕

子供の意見に耳をかさずに、親たちが勝手に縁組を結ぶこともできる、伝統ある習慣。ひとつ屋根の下で男女が他人のように別々な生活を送るように仕組むものだと言う人もいる。しかし、そんな結婚生活も意外と成立するのだ！

《相親》

日本的傳統之一，由家中長輩主導安排的牽紅線儀式，子女不能有意見。有些人認爲這個習俗的設計是讓夫妻在結婚前，先適應如同陌生人的生活方式，但有時竟然很成功。

Omiai (The Arranged Marriage)

A classic native custom which allows for elderly members of the species to decide the pairing arrangements in a way where the offspring get no say in the matter. Some observers believe this custom is designed to allow the couple to lead completely separate lives under the same roof but sometimes it works!

〔ガソリンスタンドの女子店員〕

必要以上に陽気で頼まれてもいないのに車の窓を磨く。彼女たちは全員、姉妹やイトコ同士だと思われる――みな同じ顔をしているのだ。客の車が入ると出迎え、出ていく時は「ありがとう」を連呼するのはわかる。しかし、身を挺してまで車を渋滞道路に割り込ませる手伝いをするのはスゴイ。

《加油站女孩》

　　超出想像的親切爽朗，不等你開口就會把車窗擦乾淨。這個族群似乎彼此間都有姐妹親戚關係，因為看起來都是一個樣子。她們不僅歡迎客人來加油，客人離去時，除了報以熱烈的感謝外，更有一招是挺身而出，擋住車陣，幫你重新上路。

Gas Station Girl

Always cheerful, will clean windows without being asked. These members of the species appear to be all related to one another because they all look the same. They will welcome you upon arrival and not only gush thanks on your departure but will hold up traffic to allow you to get your car back into the traffic jam.

〔ヤキトリ屋のオヤジ〕

くつ箱ほどの大きさの店を構えて、炭火の煙にいぶされながら、トリのとても口では言えないような部位の肉を焼いている。店の壁や柱は油でギトギトなのに、客席はきれいになっているのが不思議。トリの脂肪の焦げるにおいで、すぐに居所がかぎわけられる人々。

《串烤店的老闆》

　　隨處可見，通常攤位不大，在如鞋盒般大小的店裡，彎著腰在燒烤架前翻烤著一串串雞和豬身上難以啓口的部位。小店的牆壁和樑柱上經常蒙著一層油垢，但客人用餐的座位卻異常的乾淨。只要順著空氣中聞到的烤雞香味，憑著嗅覺應該可以馬上找到。

Yakitori Chef

This breed can be found all over the place, usually in shoe box sized stores, hunched over a brazier while they barbecue indescribable bits of chicken or pig. Their nests are often coated in a layer of grease although the serving areas are squeaky clean. Can be found by sniffing the air for burning chicken fat.

〔落語家〕
　この人種は、長時間正座をしながらしゃべりまくることができる。日本人は彼らの話に腹をかかえて笑う。落語家のコンテストもある。しかし、日本語のわかるガイジンでも、彼らの面白さはなかなかわからない。日本語のシャレやオチは伝わりにくいようだ。

《「落語家」（相聲）》
　　這個族群有能耐跪坐好幾個鐘頭，同時嘴巴說個不停。在這般的「脫口秀」之中，常令人捧腹大笑。同時還會舉行競賽。但是對多數懂日語的外國人而言，常搞不懂好笑在那裡。可能是因日語中的特殊俏皮話和落語特有的結束語等無法貼切的傳達之故。

The Story Teller

This breed is capable of sitting on its heels for hours and talking continuously. They are considered screamingly funny by other members of the species and often take part in contests. To many foreigners who understand the language, their tales are not the least bit funny. Japanese nuance doesn't translate.

〔白マスクの男〕

冬がやってくると、この連中が台頭する。真冬には電車やバスに乗り合わせた人のうち5〜6人は必ずコレである。あまりしゃべらず、やたら咳やくしゃみをする。外科用メスの持ち方や傷口の縫い合わせ方を知っている者は皆無に等しいのに、なぜ医療用マスクをしているのか不可解。

《白口罩男人》

　　只要一進入冬季，這個族群就會出現。在嚴冬時節電車或是巴士上至少有5~6位。他們不太說話，但經常咳嗽及打噴嚏。這些人幾乎沒有一個知道要如何使用手術刀，更別提傷口縫合技巧，真納悶他們為什麼要戴著醫療用的口罩。

The White Surgical Masked Man

As winter closes in, this breed begins to appear. By mid winter there are at least half a dozen on every form of public transport. They don't talk much and appear to cough and sneeze a lot. Nearly all of them would not know which end of a scalpel to pick up, let alone how to tie a knot in a suture.

〔野球ボールの巣〕

未来の野球選手たちがホームラン王になるための神殿と言われていたが、都会に鳥がほとんどいない今では、鳥の巣にボールが収まっている光景も珍しくなりつつある。ボールがここで孵化したという記録はないし、実際持ち主が取り戻しに行ったということもない——大抵の木は枝が切られていて登れないのだ。

《棒球巢》

從前的人相信把棒球放在鳥巢，加以膜拜的話，據說可以使未來的棒球選手成為全壘打王，但是因為都市中鳥類日益稀少，所以這種棒球巢也愈來愈少見。並無相關記載說明這種球是否被孵化或者實際上是由主人取回。因為樹枝大多被砍掉了，因此很難爬上樹去查證。

Baseball Nest

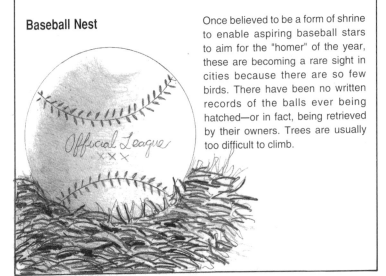

Once believed to be a form of shrine to enable aspiring baseball stars to aim for the "homer" of the year, these are becoming a rare sight in cities because there are so few birds. There have been no written records of the balls ever being hatched—or in fact, being retrieved by their owners. Trees are usually too difficult to climb.

〔チカン〕

　触わりたくなるような柔らかい羽毛のメンドリやヒヨコたちの群れに、好んで入っていく人種。この国の女性は、このようなイカガワシイ行為に対して大声で抵抗することが少ないので、バイ菌のごとくはびこっている。外国でこんなことをしようものなら、針のようなハイヒールで思いっきり足を踏まれるか、目のまわりに青アザをつくるのがオチである。

《色狼（痴漢）》

　經常伸出「祿山之爪」去撫摸母鳥或是雛鳥的柔軟羽毛，因此常擠入女性群體中，大吃豆腐。由於受侵犯的日本女性很少會大聲表示抗議，使得這個族類有如細菌般的大量繁殖。在國外這些色狼的行為若不是會被高跟鞋狠狠踹上一腳，最少也會讓他的眼睛多一個黑眼圈。

The Chikan

Usually migrate into flocks of hens and chicks where there are ample tail feathers to caress. It is believed that there are more of these than meet the eye due to the fact that females of the species rarely complain aloud about this form of harassment. The occasional Chikan who plies his trade overseas will either get a stiletto heel through his foot or at very least a black eye.

〔カラスとハト〕

都会に住む唯一の鳥類。道ばたにあまりゴミがない日本では、この鳥たちはコンクリートやアスファルト、それにタバコの吸いがらを主食にしていると言われる。とにかく、排気ガスを吸って生きているのは事実。ふだんは恐れ多いほど静かだが、人々が日曜日の朝寝坊を決めこんだとたん、きまってギャーギャーと耳をつんざく不敵な鳥でもある。

《烏鴉與鴿子》

　　生存在都市中僅有的鳥類。由於日本街上幾乎找不到垃圾，有些人深信牠們是以混凝土、瀝青和煙屁股爲主食。至少事實上牠們每天都吸著汽車排放的廢氣。牠們通常安靜得令人生畏，但當星期天早上你想睡個懶覺時，牠們偏偏會變得非常吵，哇！哇！刺耳地叫個不停。

Crows and Pigeons

The only winged population of all cities. Due to the comparatively low level of rubbish in the streets, some observers believe these birds can eat concrete, bitumen and cigarette butts. It is certain however that they can breath photochemical fog. They are usually silent and awesome until you want to sleep in on a Sunday morning when they will invariably become raucous and a pain in the ear.

〔名刺交換の儀式〕

　男性の服装に自己表現のないこの国では、初対面の男同士が相手のステイタスを知るために欠かせないもの。この儀式を行ってから、お辞儀の角度や言葉づかいを決める。座ってからも、相手の名前を忘れないよう、テーブルに名刺を置いたまま話を続ける。

《交換名片的儀式》

　　在男性的服裝上無法表現自己個性的這個國家，初見面時，男士們必須藉著交換名片得知彼此的身份地位。舉行這種儀式之後，決定鞠躬的角度及所用客套話的型態。就坐後，還得把收到的名片依序放在面前的桌上，以便記住對方的名字，繼續談話。

The Card Exchange Ritual

In a land where male plumage doesn't vary, this ritual is performed upon first meeting any other male as a means of discovering status. Then, the angle of bow and the type of language to be used are preset according to ancient protocol. The cards received are fanned out in front of one so one can remember just whom the other people are.

〔学者（がくしゃ）〕

スピーチができると聞（き）けば、結婚式（けっこんしき）だろうが公共（こうきょう）機関（きかん）だろうが、どこにでも現（あらわ）れる、非常（ひじょう）におしゃべりで退屈（たいくつ）な人種（じんしゅ）。国営（えい）（？）放送（ほうそう）は彼（かれ）らを頻繁（ひんぱん）に出演（しゅつえん）させ、日経（にっけい）インデックスの上昇（じょうしょう）・下降（かこう）から、英国王室（えいこくおうしつ）の賛否（さんぴ）にいたるもろもろの閑話（かんわ）をさせている。

《學者》

只要聽說那裡能夠發表演講，不論是婚禮或公共場合，這個族群一定出現，喜好發言但經常是些無聊的說辭。全國電視網總是請他們談論大小事件，從分析日經指數漲跌的原因到英國皇室的流言蜚語。

The Scholar

Very talkative and often quite boring, this species appears on a rostrum at every wedding or public function. National TV always invites them to speak about everything from why the NIKKEI index rises/falls to what is right/wrong about the British Royal family.

〔幸福な通勤族〕

新聞を広げるスペースのある座席に、いつも陣取っている。ということは、電車の中で生まれた人々らしい。読んでいる記事に憤慨しているように見えるのは、応援する野球チームが連敗しているからにすぎない場合が多い。つねに背広姿。

《快樂的通勤族》

在通勤電車上總是有座位，而且很自然就有足夠的空間讓他們攤開報紙閱讀，想必都是在電車上出生的幸運兒吧。當他們對所看的內容面露惱怒之色時，往往可能只是他們最喜歡的棒球隊連吃敗仗的時候。這種族群都是身穿西裝者爲多。

The Happy Commuter

This breed is probably born on the trains because they always have a seat, which automatically gives them enough space to open a newspaper. Appear to be seething internally at what they read, but it is usually only a sign that their favorite baseball team is on a losing streak. Always in a suit.

〔レッサー・パンダ〕

明るくかわいく無邪気だが、それ以外はジャイアントパンダにはほとんど似ていない。この動物には、誰とでも臆面なく話し、ところかまわず図々しく遊ぶ術がある。そんな資質を生かして、大人になるとディズニーランドで働いたり政治家になる者もいるようだが、たいていはサラリーマンやOLになる。

《小貓熊》

　　除了可愛、無憂無慮討人喜歡的特質外，與大貓熊完全不像。這種族群擅於在陌生人面前表達意見，善於交際而毫不腆覥。長大後少數到狄斯耐樂園上班，當然有些會成為政治家，但多數成為普通的上班族。

The Lesser Panda

Delightful, cute and cuddly, but beyond these attributes, bear little resemblance to the giant panda. This species learns how to speak and can often be seen playing in the company of different species without being at all shy. When older, sometimes join Disneyland but most become salarymen or OL's. It is believed, some become politicians.

〔白いシッポのテニスプレーヤー〕

オリの中を好み、どんな公営コートにもたくさんいる。両手打ちが得意な点、それにオリのまわりに１００個ほどのボールを散乱させる点なども特徴。飛んできた球を打つ時の表情は深刻そのもので、不気味なほど黙々とプレーする人々。

《穿著白色褲裙的網球族》

　　從早到晚在多數公營球場都可看見這類喜歡在網球籠內的族群。大部份擅長雙手揮拍，且往往至少有一百個球散落在其腳邊。面對來球，擊球時看似極度認真，所以很少閒話家常。

The White Tailed Tennis Player

A caged member of the species seen at most municipal centers from dawn to dusk. Often use both hands to swing their rackets and have at least 100 balls scattered around their cage. Always look extremely serious when actually hitting an airborne ball and rarely talk to each other.

〔「ハーフ」の子供たち〕

日本人とガイジンの親から生まれたので、この国ではそう呼ばれている子供たち。しかし実は、彼らは独自の人種なのだ。その多くが二つの言語と二つの文化を完全に理解し、どんな国の食べ物も食べられ、物事を二面的に見て、人生を楽しむ術を持つ。他の人間より数倍アタマもよかったりする。というわけで、「ハーフ」ではなく「ダブル」と呼ぶにふさわしい存在なのである。

《混血兒》

日本人和外國人所生的小孩，在日本被稱爲「Half」，往往自成一個族群。通常具雙語能力且深受兩國文化薰陶，能接受各國型態的食物，從不同的角度觀察事情，能以異於常人的能力去發現新事物，聰明才智兩倍於同儕，所以他們應改名爲「Double」。

The "WAA" Children

Nicknamed "Half" children by the natives because these are the offspring of one Japanese and one foreign parent, these inhabitants are a species on their own. Usually totally bicultural and bilingual, they can eat any type of food, see situations from two different sides, have twice the capacity to find things amusing and are often more than two times as bright as many of their contemporaries. They should be renamed "Double" children.

〔日本人ウォッチャー〕

ガイジン（日本人と結婚している場合が多い）。日本人は喜んで彼らを受け入れているというより、黙認しているようである。左利きでハシを使えば面白がられ、タクワンや納豆を食べれば意外な顔をされ、ちょっとでも日本語を話せば腰を抜かして驚かれる。若い頃は日本人や日本社会を自分が変えようとやっきになったが、今ではただニンマリと笑って事態をながめるばかりだ。

《鳥類觀察家》

是指在日本的外國人，多數已和日本女人結婚。不過並不代表他們受到歡迎，通常只是被日本人默認接受。他們以左手拿筷或吃著日本式的醃蘿蔔及納豆等食物時會讓日本人覺得有趣和驚訝，稍微露兩兩句日語時更讓日本人目瞪口呆。年輕時試圖要改變日本人和日本社會，如今卻只有一笑置之，靜觀事態轉變。

The Observers

Foreigners (married to native lasses) who are often simply tolerated rather than accepted into the species. Will amaze some folk when they use chopsticks lefthanded or eat ethnic food and dumbfound all by occasionally mumbling oaths in Japanese. Used to try to change the system but now, just smile a lot.

“ 日 本 鳥 人 ”

中華民國 87 年 3 月 1 日再版 2 刷發行　　　　定價新台幣180元整

發行人：張　思　本
發行所：漢思有限公司
　　　　台北市敦化南路二段 1 號 7 樓
　　　　T E L：(02) 2705-5848
　　　　F A X：(02) 2702-0365
郵撥帳號：　18418738
登記證：新聞局局版台業字第6441號

總經銷：知遠文化事業有限公司
電　話：(02) 2939-6007

國立中央圖書館出版品預行編目資料

日本鳥人 / Tim Ernst , Mike Marklew「原著」；
　鄺宗明譯. -- 初版. -- 台北市：漢思發行
：知遠總經銷，民 84
　面；　　公分. --（日本系列叢書；3）
譯自： The Japanese ：a field guide
ISBN 957-99695-3-1（精裝）

　1. 日本語言 - 讀本　　2. 日本 - 文化

803.18　　　　　　　　　　　　84008778